HOMETOWN HEARTS

A Mother's Homecoming

New York Times Bestselling Author
TANYA MICHAELS

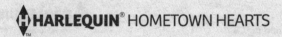

HARLEQUIN® HOMETOWN HEARTS

Recycling programs
for this product may
not exist in your area.

ISBN-13: 978-0-373-21454-9

A Mother's Homecoming

Printed in U.S.A.

www.Harlequin.com

Tanya Michaels, a *New York Times* bestselling author and five-time RITA® Award nominee, has been writing love stories since middle-school algebra class—which probably explains her math grades. Her books, praised for their poignancy and humor, have received awards from readers and reviewers alike. Tanya is an active member of Romance Writers of America and a frequent public speaker. She lives outside Atlanta with her very supportive husband, two highly imaginative kids and a bichon frise who thinks she's the center of the universe.

HOMETOWN HEARTS

SHIPMENT 1

Stranger in Town by Brenda Novak
Baby's First Homecoming by Cathy McDavid
Her Surprise Hero by Abby Gaines
A Mother's Homecoming by Tanya Michaels
A Firefighter in the Family by Trish Milburn
Tempted by a Texan by Mindy Neff

SHIPMENT 2

It Takes a Family by Victoria Pade
The Sheriff of Heartbreak County by Kathleen Creighton
A Hometown Boy by Janice Kay Johnson
The Renegade Cowboy Returns by Tina Leonard
Unexpected Bride by Lisa Childs
Accidental Hero by Loralee Lillibridge

SHIPMENT 3

An Unlikely Mommy by Tanya Michaels
Single Dad Sheriff by Lisa Childs
In Protective Custody by Beth Cornelison
Cowboy to the Rescue by Trish Milburn
The Ranch She Left Behind by Kathleen O'Brien
Most Wanted Woman by Maggie Price
A Weaver Wedding by Allison Leigh

SHIPMENT 4

A Better Man by Emilie Rose
Daddy Protector by Jacqueline Diamond
The Road to Bayou Bridge by Liz Talley
Fully Engaged by Catherine Mann
The Cowboy's Secret Son by Trish Milburn
A Husband's Watch by Karen Templeton

SHIPMENT 5

His Best Friend's Baby by Molly O'Keefe
Caleb's Bride by Wendy Warren
Her Sister's Secret Life by Pamela Toth
Lori's Little Secret by Christine Rimmer
High-Stakes Bride by Fiona Brand
Hometown Honey by Kara Lennox

SHIPMENT 6

Reining in the Rancher by Karen Templeton
A Man to Rely On by Cindi Myers
Your Ranch or Mine? by Cindy Kirk
Mother in Training by Marie Ferrarella
A Baby for the Bachelor by Victoria Pade
The One She Left Behind by Kristi Gold
Her Son's Hero by Vicki Essex

SHIPMENT 7

Once and Again by Brenda Harlen
Her Sister's Fiance by Teresa Hill
Family at Stake by Molly O'Keefe
Adding Up to Marriage by Karen Templeton
Bachelor Dad by Roxann Delaney
It's That Time of Year by Christine Wenger

SHIPMENT 8

The Rancher's Christmas Princess by Christine Rimmer
Their Baby Miracle by Lillian Darcy
Mad About Max by Penny McCusker
No Ordinary Joe by Michelle Celmer
The Soldier's Baby Bargain by Beth Kery
A Texan Under the Mistletoe by Leah Vale

Chapter One

As part of her long overdue efforts to become a better person, Pamela Jo Wilson tried to find something positive about every situation. Right now the closest thing to a silver lining she could muster was: *The car will probably break down before I get there.* She could hope, anyway.

Or maybe the balding tires would simply melt in the muggy August heat, a painfully plausible scenario.

Even with the windows rolled down, heat-stroke seemed imminent. The air-conditioning in her four-door compact had died last year, mere blocks from the used-car lot. She'd known better than to try to get a refund. In that neighborhood, she'd been lucky to get title and registration. But the dilapidated automobile had proven as stubborn as its owner, persevering all the way from California to the delta.

Now, Mississippi sun beat through her windshield with enough intensity to make her feel like an ant on the frying end of a juvenile delinquent's magnifying glass. Though Pam wasn't enjoying the heat—or the periodic stench of baked marshes and paper mills—she grudgingly appreciated the simple majesty of the azure sky above the rural stretches of untamed land she'd passed. Perfect, fluffy clouds dotted the horizon, looking more like they were from a painting than real life.

As her car chugged up the incline, a cheery wooden sign came into view. The paint job was so flawlessly fresh that she imagined some civic-minded volunteer in coveralls at the side of the road at dawn each day applying touchups with a can of aldermen-approved acrylic. Enjoy Your Stay in Beautiful Mimosa. Perfectly welcoming. Yet every molecule in Pam's body shrieked, "Turn the heck around!"

Giving up swearing was a result of step number four. It had been dam… *Darn* difficult. But she'd done it, examined her many flaws and resolved to change. With a little bit of persistence and a whole lot of divine intervention, she could do this, too. When she'd left Mimosa almost thirteen years ago, sneaking away in the night to catch a Memphis-bound bus, she'd only imagined *one* scenario that could bring her back. The long dead fantasy now seemed both laughable and petty.

Having been assured her entire youth that she had "the voice of an angel," she'd entertained a vindictive daydream of returning as—she tried not to wince, the memory felt so foolish—a country music superstar. She'd pictured arriving in town, a chart-topping American sweetheart, with just enough time in her packed schedule for a charitable concert and a shrug of indifference toward her mother...who would naturally beg forgiveness for all that had passed between them.

There was only one aspect of reality that even distantly matched her childish dream. Pam was indeed making this return trip to see Mae Danvers Wilson.

No matter what form of address Pam had been required to use aloud as a kid, she'd thought of the woman by her given name rather than Mom. Mae Wilson possessed all the warmth and maternal instincts of a cottonmouth. *Oh, and you did any better?* At thirty-one, Pam was no longer as judgmental as her teen self; she had a boatload of mistakes to keep her humble. Possibly an entire fleet's worth.

Remembering some of those mistakes, including a disastrous flirtation with motherhood, Pam blinked hard. *Don't go there.* She hadn't driven this far just to come unglued and wrap her car around a white oak.

Within the official limits of Mimosa, the first two buildings were a gas station across the street that looked new and, to her right, Wade's Watering Hole, a dive older than she was. At least it had been considered a disreputable dive over a decade ago. Now the siding and roof gleamed, and parking conditions were several evolutionary steps above the previous mud pit. Of course, one couldn't make judgments based solely on an exterior. Who knew what lurked inside the belly of the beast?

Beer, she imagined with a sigh. Cold brew on tap with just enough bitterness to make a person smack her lips. And all her old friends standing in a proud line behind a teak bar— José, Jim, Jack.

Lord, she missed Jack.

Suddenly thirsty, she gripped the steering wheel and made a sharp turn toward the fill-ing station. She could get herself a soda here. Or water, even healthier. Besides, a bucket of bolts like her car needed fuel just as much as any self-respecting automobile. As she shifted into Park, her lips spasmed in a fleeting smile of apology. She should be more appreciative of the bolt bucket. It was the most valuable thing she owned, next to a blue aluminum token and an old Gibson acoustic guitar she refused to play.

Digging through road-trip debris on the passenger seat, she located a green billed cap. Her blond hair was shorter and darker than the signature fall of corn silk it had once been, but her chin-length shag was still plenty long to be gnarled by humidity and a sixty-mile-per-hour airstream.

She got out of the car, marveling that the sensation of being slapped with damp heat even registered when she was already so hot and sweaty. It was like checking on baking biscuits—that first wave of unbearable heat when you opened the oven door didn't keep you from flinching further as you leaned down into it. At the gas pump, she selected the "pay inside" option, then circled her vehicle to grab a twenty-dollar bill from the glove compartment.

Inside the station she was met with the overhead jangle of a cowbell and a nearly orgasmic blast of air-conditioning. If she stayed in town any length of time, maybe she'd apply for a job here just to bask in how cool it was. Her contented sigh reached the ears of the bearded, middle-aged man standing behind the counter a foot away.

He laughed. "Hot out there, isn't it?"

She almost stumbled, nodding in response while keeping her face averted. *Bucky?* Until he'd spoken, she hadn't recognized him, guessing him to be older than he was. She searched her memory for Bucky's real name. Travis. Travis Beem, who'd had the bad luck to enter second grade with pronouncedly crooked front teeth. They'd eventually been corrected, but the nickname followed him all the way to graduation anyway. Change was darn near impossible in sleepy, small towns.

She remembered the day at lunch when he'd asked her to junior prom, his expression sheepish.

"It's not like I expect you to say yes—the whole school knows you'll go with Nick—but Tully bet me five bucks I wouldn't have the guts to ask." He'd grinned boyishly. *"And I could use the five bucks."*

Of course, the whole school had known she

would be at the dance with Nick. She and Nick Shepard had been inseparable back then. If she wanted to, even all these years later, she could easily recall the exact timbre of his laugh, the scent of his cologne lingering on the lettered jacket she'd so often worn. Her stomach clenched and she shoved away the encroaching memories.

Thank God he lives in North Carolina.

Facing her mother would be unpleasant, but Pam had promised herself and her sponsor, Annabel, that she would go through with it. If she'd thought there was a risk of seeing Nick Shepard, however, Pam never would have willingly set foot in the state of Mississippi. And not just for her own self-preservation, but for Nick's as well. Gwendolyn Shepard's accusation echoed in her mind. *Don't you think you've done my son enough damage?*

Pam grabbed a bottle of water from the cooler against the far wall and took it to the register. Her stomach growled when she passed a display of candy bars and potato chips, but snacks were a luxury item. Maybe the possibility of food at Mae's house would keep her motivated to finish her journey.

Eyes down, she slid her cash across the counter to Travis. "Put whatever's left after the water on pump two, please."

"Sure th—" At his abrupt halt, she reflexively raised her gaze, immediately wishing she hadn't.

His dark eyes widened.

Oh, no. She wasn't naive enough to think she could be in her hometown without people finding out, people recognizing her, but she hadn't expected it to happen so soon. *Annabel was wrong, I'm not ready.*

"Uh, sure thing," Travis finally said. He glanced out the window to where her heap sat, lowering the property value just by being there.

"Thanks." She turned to go. With concerted effort, she kept from sprinting like some over-age Ole Miss student trying out for the Rebel's track and field team. After all, the one thing she'd learned in the last twelve and a half years was that she couldn't outrun her past—not at any speed.

Behind her, Travis called, "You have a nice day, Pamela Jo."

Too late.

It wasn't that you *couldn't* go home again, Pam thought as her car bounced in the exact same pothole that used to make Nick's vintage

Mustang stutter after their dates. *You just have to be crazy or desperate to do it.* In her case, both.

But maybe people with closer-knit families viewed revisiting their roots in a different light.

She turned onto the long and winding gravel driveway. The Wilson mailbox was the same faded, ugly mustard yellow. An enduring copse of trees still blocked the view of the house from the road. However, the weeping willow that had once been at the front of the wild and unruly yard was gone.

Mae's 1980 LTD Crown Victoria was parked in the carport attached to the brick two-bedroom home; the rusted vehicle clearly hadn't been roadworthy in some time. Pam leaned forward, staring through her windshield. The car wasn't the only thing in a state of disrepair. Instead of curtains or the familiar living room suite visible through the house's grimy windows, there were large flat boards blocking further view. The concrete slab generously called a front porch had cracked, and flower-topped weeds flourished in the fissures. Several roof shingles had fallen atop neglected shrubs, and another hung precariously, as if it were barely holding on and planned to give up the ghost at any minute.

Pam knew the feeling.

She parked the car, sagging back against her

seat. Defeat and relief swirled in a bitter cocktail. Mae didn't live here.

No one lived here. It didn't appear as though the house had been sold, what with the Victoria parked in its habitual spot. If not for the deliberately boarded windows, she might have worried Mae had simply slipped and broken her fool neck with no one the wiser. Pam experienced a rare twinge of regret that she and her mother hadn't kept up *some* sort of communication over the years… Christmas greetings, postcards, hate mail with a return address.

Had her mother moved into the nursing home in Mimosa? Surely not. Although the woman's lifestyle had probably aged her prematurely, she was only in her fifties. Had she perhaps moved in with her pursed-lip, disapproving older sister, Aunt Julia? Pam shuddered at what that household would be like. *Poor Uncle Ed.*

Pam opened her car door, though she wasn't sure why she felt the need for a closer look at her childhood home. She didn't have a key. Breaking in to the tiny residence would be relatively simple but also relatively pointless. She doubted she'd find more than spiders and field mice. Why waste time here when she should be tracking down Mae? As much as the thought of talking to her mother ripped at the lining of

Pam's stomach, that's what she had come all this way to do.

During a discussion with Annabel about making amends, she'd groused in a moment of self-pity that it was too bad Mae had never joined the program because *there* was a woman with some amends to make. No-nonsense Annabel had pointed out in her wry, get-a-clue way that hating Mae was damaging Pam far more than her estranged mother.

Pam had decided that if she couldn't get forgiveness from the people she'd hurt—Nick's face flashed in her mind—the next best thing she could do was to forgive the person who'd hurt her. Maybe once Pam made peace with her mother, she could truly move forward. Because right now, Pam's life was as much in shambles as this pitiful little house.

Kicking a rock out of her path, she stepped closer. The room on the corner closest to her was the kitchen. The majority of meals in Pam's childhood had consisted of cereal or microwaved entrées. Every once in a great while Mae had cooked up something fantastic, mostly to impress new boyfriends when she was sober enough to care. There had been one guy, a truck driver, who'd returned to them again and again for an entire winter. He'd taught Pam how to play guitar. It had been one of the happiest seasons of her life. She had fond memories of strumming in the living room and losing herself in the discovery of new chords.

Bittersweet were the later memories of that same living room when she and Nick, juniors in high school, had lost their virginity together on the couch. They'd been kids, completely inept at what they were doing. Yet how many times in the years since had she wished she could once again sink into his embrace, those arms made muscular by football practices, and made safe by his love?

According to Nick's mother—furious that Pam had the gall to phone after all these years, even if it was only to get contact information for an apology—Nick was happily remarried and raising his daughter in North Carolina. *Our daughter.* Pam's chest squeezed so tightly she couldn't breathe. Finally a harsh sob grated out, opening up her airway and allowing her to inhale in jagged, hiccupy breaths.

The sound startled a group of grackle in the tree above her. She couldn't help envying their escape as they took to the air. One stubborn bird maintained its perch, narrowing its beady black eyes as if to challenge, *Now what?*

Excellent question.

* * *

Pam had been on the way to Aunt Julia and Uncle Ed's when her car overheated. As proof that there was indeed a God, the car sputtered to a stop right across the street from Granny K's Kitchen. Pam wondered if Granny K's, a venerable town institution, still served the best chicken-fried steak known to man.

Technically she shouldn't be splurging on dinner or she'd be broke by the end of the week. Then again, she was supposed to be taking life one day at a time. Besides, Annabel had admonished more than once that Pam was "damn near skeletal." A gravy-laden meal from Granny K's while the car cooled down would be good for both Pam and the vehicle.

Granny K's was the type of establishment where you seated yourself. Within minutes, Pam had placed an order for chicken-fried steak and a side of mashed potatoes. Although the menus had been redesigned, she was thrilled to see all her favorite dishes still remained.

The platinum-haired waitress—Helen, according to the unevenly spaced letters on a white plastic rectangle—bobbed her head in acknowledgment of Pam's order. "I'll be right back with your glass of water, hon."

"Wait." Pam surprised herself with a burst

of curiosity. "The original owner, Kat McAdams? Does she still run the place?" Pam had no real sense of the proprietor's age. When Pam was a teenager, Kat had seemed ancient, but anyone over twenty-five had seemed that way. Now that Pam thought about it, she doubted Kat had been anywhere old enough for granny status back then.

Helen narrowed her hazel eyes, assessing. "You from around here?"

"A long time ago, yeah."

"Then you don't know about the stroke? Kat recovered, but the doctors told her she had to slow down. She has a room over at Magnolia Hills Senior Community, but she's in here at least once a week to make sure everything's shipshape. She sold part ownership to Davy Lowe, but he didn't come in to oversee dinner shift tonight because his champion beagle is supposed to have her pups."

"Thank you." Pam had cut all ties with Mimosa the night she left; the relatively impersonal inquiry about Kat McAdams was a low-risk way of easing back into her past life. It was unexpectedly reassuring to know that Granny K was alive and kicking and still looking out for her diner.

Helen moved to the next table, greeting a

young couple and their boisterous toddler, and Pam surveyed the diner. The setup hadn't changed much over the years, although the color scheme—formerly red and white—had been altered to a deep green and softer ivory. Additional booths had been installed toward the back where there had once been a jukebox and a coin-operated air-hockey table. During her perusal of the surroundings, Pam noticed that a young woman—maybe early twenties—was staring at her. Pam couldn't understand why. The stranger seemed too young to be anyone from Pam's past. *And too old to be Faith.*

Swallowing, Pam pushed away the thought. If she kept picking at emotional scabs, she would never heal.

Suddenly she realized that the other woman had stood and she looked as if she were coming this way. Crap, for all Pam knew, Mae had remarried and this girl was her stepsister. But before the stranger had taken two steps, another woman ducked into Pam's line of sight and the twentysomething altered course.

"Why, Pamela Jo, that *is* you," a tiny redhead drawled.

Pam tensed, feeling ridiculously vulnerable without her baseball cap and no food yet to occupy her attention or make her look busy.

Luckily the woman already cheerfully seating herself on the other side of the table seemed friendly. She wore a sleeveless floral dress and barely topped five feet—not exactly the intimidating type. If she managed to break a hundred pounds, it would be because the heavy cloud of auburn framing her face tipped her over the edge. Pam forced her expression into an answering smile.

"Yep. It's me. But I just go by Pam now."

The woman winked, conspiratorial. "Now that we're all grown up, hmm? Well, I'm still Violet, same as I ever was."

Violet Keithley. Pam blinked, reacclimating to yet another piece of her past rising up to meet her. "Sure, I remember you." They'd been in different grades, not close at all, but Violet had been a member of church choir with her. Backup soprano, not one of the frequent soloists like Pam.

"It's so nice to see you again." Violet shook her head, setting the voluminous mass in motion. "I always expected I'd turn on the radio one day and hear your voice."

"Yeah, well… So are you here tonight with your family? Husband, kids?" Pam was more than willing to coo appreciatively over wallet-sized pictures of Violet's children if it meant not having to talk about herself.

"Oh, no." Violet tittered. "Haven't found the right guy to make an honest woman of me yet. My sister, Cora, got married last June and told me I should take up fishing to meet men. That's how she did it."

At the image of ultrapetite Violet wrestling a bass out of the Yazoo River, Pam fought a grin.

"I was going to meet one of my friends for dinner," Violet continued, "but she called when I was already halfway here to say her little boy is feeling funny. He doesn't usually mind staying with his daddy, but you know how it is. Everyone wants Mama when they're sick."

Not everyone.

Almost as soon as Pam formed the sardonic thought—born more of habit than heat—she reconsidered. Alcoholism was an illness and, as part of her attempted recovery, here she was seeking Mae.

The waitress returned with two glasses of water and offered a menu to Violet, who glanced questioningly across the table. Pam shrugged. Violet was harmless enough and no doubt could fill in some of the blanks about life in Mimosa since Pam's departure.

"You mentioned mothers," Pam said awkwardly once the waitress had gone with Violet's order. "Do you, um, remember mine?" Colorful at best and a drunken home-wrecker at worst, Mae was nothing if not memorable. Pam felt the best way to bring the woman into conversation was slowly. No telling how many townsfolk had legitimate axes to grind.

"Mae Wilson. Of course." Surprisingly Violet's expression softened. "My condolences on her passing."

"Passing?" The clatter of the diner fell away, drowned out by the pounding in Pam's ears. Although she'd earlier allowed the snarky thought about Mae breaking her neck inside her house—which now struck her as in incredibly poor taste—she hadn't for a second believed it. Mae had once totaled a boyfriend's car and walked away without a scratch on her.

Besides, this was her mother. Wasn't there some sort of psychic umbilical cord? The woman who had brought her into this world and raised her had died. Ceased to exist. Wouldn't Pam have experienced at least a minor twinge?

Maybe you were too wasted to notice the twinge.

Violet pressed a hand to her heart, and Pam lip-read her words more than heard them.

"You didn't know? My God. I'm so sorry. I thought..."

Blindly, Pam grabbed the glass in front of her and instinctively tossed some of its contents down her throat. Instead of the burn of whiskey she still half expected on some base, cellular level, there was only tepid water. It took her a moment to reorient.

Right, she didn't drink whiskey anymore.

And Mae Danvers Wilson wasn't alive anymore.

I'm too late.

Perhaps it was hypocritical to feel devastated by the loss of a mother she'd barely known even when they shared a house. Having not interacted with Mae in years, it was silly to think that not doing so now would truly affect her day-to-day life. But to drive all this way, to have rehearsed and rehashed and wondered for hundreds of miles how her olive branch would be received...

"Wh-what happened?" Pam's question seemed to echo from a distance.

"I heard liver failure." Violet ducked her gaze. "I'm so sorry, Pam. I knew you didn't make it back in time for the funeral, but... Earlier this summer your aunt and uncle hired someone to find you. I thought maybe that's what brought you to town."

"My aunt and uncle." Pam swallowed. "They were going to be my next stop after dinner."

"The Calberts?" Violet was practically trembling with discomfort, her gaze darting around as if she wished she could flee. "Oh, honey, they're not home. Your aunt was gone for a long weekend, one of those craft shows she does in the next county. I know because Cora's been watering all their outside plants while... Listen to me prattling on. I'm so—"

"No, it's fine," Pam said. But of course it wasn't. What a horrible thing to say. Her mother was dead and she was blurting "it's fine"? She just hadn't wanted Violet to keep apologizing.

"I think they're getting back tomorrow sometime," Violet offered.

Pam bit her lip. "Could you maybe recommend a good place for me to stay the night?" Should she admit what kind of budget she was on? No doubt that would elicit more pity.

"A couple of those big hotel chains have places out by the highway."

"I was thinking more...quaint."

"Well, Trudy rents rooms, by the night or longer, in that faux mansion of hers on Meadowberry. She's probably got a couple of vacancies. Although…"

"Although what?" Pam prompted reluctantly. From the way Violet was squirming in her seat, it couldn't be good.

"Excuse me, ladies." Helen reached between them to set down two steaming plates of food. Too bad Pam had entirely lost her appetite. "Can I get y'all anything else?"

Pam shook her head mutely, waiting for the other shoe to drop. She tried to take comfort in the fact that no matter what Violet's next words were, they could hardly compare to the shocking news of Mae's death.

When the waitress bustled off, Violet attempted an unconvincing smile. "Mmm. Nothing like Granny K's home cookin', is there?"

"Before we were interrupted, you were going to tell me something?"

Violet toyed with the lacy collar on her dress. "Now, I don't want to speak out of turn—Cora always scolds about me being a gossip—but it's no secret that you and Nick Shepard used to—"

"Nick?" The world tilted with nauseating speed, the way it had on mornings she'd tried to stand up too fast with a hangover. "What about him?"

"He lives on Meadowberry, too. Kind of across the street from Trudy. With his daughter."

"F-Faith is in town?" Nothing was right in the universe. Her mother was suddenly unexpectedly gone, and her daughter—who had supposedly relocated to North Carolina—was here? *I have no right to be within ten counties of that poor kid.* If you looked up *unfit* in the dictionary, there'd be a picture of Pam. It seemed to be a female family legacy, one she had vowed would stop with her.

Belatedly, the other half of what Violet said clicked. Tiny black spots obscured Pam's vision as the blood drained from her face.

Nick was in Mimosa.

Chapter Two

If this evening was a sign of what the teen-age years were going to be like, Nick Shepard should go out right now and buy up the pharmacy's aspirin supply. Maybe he could get some kind of bulk discount. He'd have to drag his mutinous twelve-and-a-half-year-old daughter along with him to the store rather than leave her here because apparently she couldn't be trusted.

He and Faith were currently having dinner, seated side by side on high-backed stools at the breakfast bar—a habit that drove his mother crazy. "You have a perfectly nice kitchen table, Nicholas," his mother would say. "I don't un-derstand why you insist on eating at the counter as if this were some low-budget diner." For once, he found himself wishing that they were at the table. If Faith were sitting across from him, it might be easier to read what was going on in that tween brain of hers.

As it was, she kept her head bent over the plate. She scraped her fork across the ceramic at discordant intervals but didn't actually eat anything. Her dark hair—the only visible trait she'd inherited from him—hung down, obscuring her features and shutting him out.

They'd always been so close, but lately...

He sighed, determined to try again. "Can you explain to me, rationally, why you're the one who's angry? You're a good kid, so you know what you did was wrong and that grounding you for the upcoming weekend is probably less than you deserve. Your grandmom and aunt Leigh already think I'm too soft on you."

From behind the curtain of Faith's wavy hair, he could swear he actually *heard* her eyes roll.

"Why can't they just butt out?" she grumbled.

He occasionally had that same thought. But then he remembered that, technically, he'd blown two marriages and his daughter needed some female influence in her life to counterbalance the rough-edged construction workers

Nick employed. "If you want them to interfere less," he suggested, "stop proving them right!"

"You act like I got caught running a meth lab. I missed one lousy class."

"A math class! I thought you wanted to take advanced math courses when you get to high school." He would like to claim that her skill with arithmetic came from him, but truthfully, it dovetailed with her innate gift for music—rhythm and frequency and pattern. When she sang, it was as if he were being haunted by her mother.

Pamela Jo might not be dead, but she was definitely the ghost of his past.

"It's only the second week of school, Dad. Everything's review right now. I didn't miss anything important." Suddenly Faith flipped her hair back, meeting his eyes and changing strategy. "Besides, you've always taught me the importance of loyalty and being a good friend. Morgan really needed to talk. She was so upset, that's why I bailed."

At the mention of Faith's boy-crazy best friend, Nick fought the urge to gnash his teeth. The girls weren't even in high school yet and Morgan was already dating. At the Fourth of July cookout, he'd caught Morgan in his back-yard making out with some teenage punk who should have been old enough to know better. God knew what kind of trouble Morgan would get into by graduation.

Hypocrite. He knew what kind of trouble he'd been into at that age. Which was all the more reason why he wanted Faith to expand her circle of friends.

"There's a difference between wanting to help someone and letting them drag you down with them," he said. "If you skipped class every time Morgan was upset over a boy, you'd flunk out by Christmas."

"What a jerky thing to say!"

Jerky, perhaps, but not untrue. "That's not an appropriate way to talk to your father. If—"

When the phone rang, he wasn't sure exactly which of them was being saved by the bell. He pointed to her plate while he stood to check caller ID. "Eat. We'll discuss this later. After your homework and a written apology to your math teacher."

If that was Morgan on the other end of that phone, she was in for a rude awakening. But no. Ashford, Leigh. It was his sister calling. Had she heard about Faith's trip to the principal's office today? Possibly. Leigh's husband taught eighth grade science at the middle school.

He stifled a sigh. "Hello?"

"Hey, Nicky."

Nicky? It was a childhood nickname, used now only when she was deeply concerned. He'd heard it a lot after the divorce. *How you hanging in there, Nicky? You're doing the right thing by moving back home, Nicky.* Granted, he was having a difficult afternoon, but Faith had missed class—it wasn't as if she'd set the school on fire.

"Hey, sis." He carried the cordless phone toward the living room. Call it male pride, but if his kid sister was about to lecture him on his parenting deficiencies, he didn't want to chance Faith overhearing. Halfway out of the kitchen, he circled back to collect Faith's cell phone off the island, throwing her a pointed look as he did so. Somehow the phone that had originally been purchased "for emergencies" sent and received an awful lot of texts.

"I thought you might need to talk," Leigh said hesitantly.

He frowned. It was highly unlike Leigh to be tentative, especially where Faith was concerned. Normally the women in his family lobbed their unsolicited opinions at him with all the subtlety of grenades.

"To tell the truth," he said, "I'm not much of a conversationalist right now. It's been a rough day, and I've got a pounding headache." Amazing how half an hour with a twelve-year-old girl could be more skull-crushing than a six-hour shift surrounded by jackhammers and other power tools.

"I understand," Leigh agreed. "But Nick…? However much it's against the manly men code to talk about your feelings, you're gonna need an adult to vent to. I remember how badly wrecked you were before, and Faith was just a baby then. This time, she—"

"Wait." Nick paced the living room, trying to process his sister's words. What *before* and *this time?* "You're not talking about Faith getting detention, are you?"

"She got detention!" For a second Leigh's voice rose in outrage. But then she regrouped. "Not why I phoned, one problem at a time. I assumed you'd heard because I've already got three calls from Granny K's, but… Your rough day's about to get worse, bro."

He stopped by a row of shelves where younger, sweeter Faiths grinned at him from myriad frames. "Just say it quick, Leigh. Like ripping off a bandage."

"Pamela Jo Wilson is back."

No. After almost thirteen years, he'd come to believe he'd never have to hear those words.

Squeezing his eyes shut, he leaned his head against the top shelf. Pamela Jo? Visions of handbaskets danced in his head—all plummeting straight downward and taking him along for the ride.

Pam turned the key in the ignition. While she wasn't one-hundred-percent enthusiastic about driving over to Meadowberry, she was definitely ready to leave the diner. The meal had been a dismal failure. Although Violet was too well-bred to simply bolt when the conversation had grown horribly awkward, it was as if she'd become too afraid to say anything else. She'd abruptly stopped talking, shutting the barn door after the horse had already escaped. *At which point, it broke its leg and had to be shot.*

Honestly, how could Violet have worried about making it any worse?

The two women had endured the rest of dinner in virtual silence. When Pam couldn't take any more, she'd asked for a to-go box and brought the painful evening to a close. Until her aunt and uncle returned tomorrow, her options seemed limited to renting a room at Trudy's or sleeping in her car. That's all her day needed, to be arrested for illegal loitering.

Although Pam drove by several subdivisions

with stately brick entrances and cookie-cutter houses, Meadowberry Street had been established long before any newfangled neighborhood zoning. The winding lane was dotted with an odd assortment of residences, from modest ranch houses to a rare cottage to a grandiose three-story house to a rust-sided trailer that looked like it would blow away in a strong gulf breeze.

There was no telling where Nick lived—she slouched low in her seat and steadfastly avoided reading the names on mailboxes—but Trudy's plantation-style "mansion" was unmistakable. It wasn't necessarily the biggest home, but it was far and away the most ornate with its columns and decorative arches. In the golden summer dusk, it was easy to see the place needed some paint and repair. Still, Pam would bet it was picturesque in the moonlight.

She felt a moment of kinship with the old house. *I don't look my best in direct sun anymore, either.* There were two driveways—one that curved into a horseshoe in front and a gravel drive that ran alongside the house and disappeared in the back. Maybe it had once been a servants' entrance. It took Pam safely out of sight of anyone who might be watching from across the street.

Where the driveway met the backyard, a barefoot woman in a denim housedress and wide-brimmed straw hat stood watering plants. She spun around at the sound of Pam's car, splattering the driver's side window with water. Pam waited until the hose had been safely lowered before opening her door.

"Who the hell are you?" the woman demanded in a thick accent. "You look worse than some of the half-mangled critters my cat brings into the house."

Pam was so startled she almost grinned. Apparently this little old lady hadn't received the memo about Southern hospitality. "Pam Wilson, ma'am."

The woman jerked a thumb toward herself. "Trudy. And this is my place."

"I heard in town that you sometimes rent to boarders," Pam began.

A white brow hitched in the air. "Awfully late to be dropping by unannounced in search of a room."

It was barely twilight, but since Pam didn't relish the idea of sleeping in her car, she nodded contritely. "I apologize for the hour."

Trudy sniffed. "There are four rooms upstairs, twenty-five dollars cash each. Tonight, all of them happen to be available. Ladies and married couples only. I don't house any single men traveling alone, even with Cappy for protection. And no gentleman callers!"

"Absolutely not." Pam wondered absently whether Cappy was a hound dog, husband or sawed-off shotgun.

"The bedrooms each have small private bathrooms with a shower stall, but I don't guarantee hot water." The woman tossed this comment out belligerently as if she doubted Pam were tough enough to weather a cold shower. "There's one TV, downstairs in the common area. You're free to use the microwave, but other than that, my kitchen is off-limits. I'll need to see some ID. Is there a Mimosa citizen who can vouch for you?"

"Violet Keithley is the one who recommended you," Pam said as she reached into her car for an old driver's license. Technically it hadn't expired yet, but the address was hopelessly out of date. "I just need a place to stay the night until my aunt Julia gets back tomorrow."

Trudy nodded sharply. "Well, come on then, if you're coming. In another few minutes, I'll be missing my program."

After grabbing her duffel bag and leftover chicken-fried steak from the car, Pam followed Trudy—no last name; Mimosa, Mississippi's answer to Cher and Madonna—into the house. The air-conditioning rattled through the vents in a feeble attempt to ward off the day's heat. It wasn't the cool bliss of this afternoon's gas station, but it was a vast improvement over Pam's car. In her tired, grungy state, a shower sounded like heaven, no matter what the temperature of the water.

It was a humbling commentary on her life that the cranky septuagenarian and her run-down house were easily the best things to happen to Pam today.

Nick yawned, wishing that the day's forecast called for rain. The cheery morning sunlight that filled his kitchen was doing nothing to help his headache. He estimated that between turning off the late-night sports show before bed and getting up to fix Faith eggs a couple of hours ago, he'd slept a total of…about four minutes. Thoughts of Pamela Jo Wilson had kept him awake all night.

No, he corrected himself as he chugged a third cup of coffee in the now-empty house. He hadn't been thinking about Pamela Jo, the person. He'd been over her for years. His mind had only been occupied with the possible repercussions of her visit.

Last night had been like learning a Category 3 hurricane was headed in his direction. It stood to reason that he'd spend a little time battling denial and being angry, then start planning for how best to cope. It was a damn shame he couldn't protect his daughter from Pamela Jo's presence with sandbags and an emergency supply of bottled water.

In fact, he was kicking himself even now for letting Faith go off to school unprepared. He'd wanted to learn more about Pamela Jo's intentions before he said anything to his daughter—who was barely speaking to him right now anyway. But what if she found out from a schoolmate that her mother was in town? None of her peers had ever known Pamela Jo, of course, but eventually adult gossip trickled down to the younger citizens of Mimosa.

Then you'd better deal with this immediately. Leigh had suggested he meet with a lawyer today, which he'd initially rejected as overkill.

"She left us with no more than a note," he'd pointed out bitterly, "in which she granted me full undisputed custody of our daughter. And all this time later you think she's had a change of heart and came back to Mimosa to fight me for Faith?" He couldn't picture that. In the short time Pamela Jo had lived with them, she'd had to be bullied into even holding the baby.

"She was a scared kid," Leigh had replied. It was the single most empathetic statement she'd ever uttered about his ex. "I mean, so were you, that's no excuse, and she was horrible and self-ish, but one assumes she might have regretted her actions since then. We don't know anything about what her last couple of years have been like. What if she's settled down and tried to have kids, but can't? What if she thinks Faith is her last chance at motherhood?"

Screw that. Pamela Jo forfeited any such chance a long time ago. And she was crazy if she thought to drag Faith through some sort of custody battle or belated "Mommy's home now, darling!" movie-of-the-week moment. Despite his sister's well-meaning suggestion of hiring legal counsel, Nick favored a more direct approach.

One that centered around figuring out where Pamela Jo was staying, then running her out of town on a rail.

Chapter Three

Shortly after nine in the morning, Pam's prepaid cell phone rang. The only reason she was still in bed was misplaced optimism. She hadn't managed to get any sleep the night before but kept hoping that, any minute now, slumbering oblivion would be hers.

"Hi, Annabel." She'd known who was on the other end before she even pressed "accept call." No one but her sponsor had the number. The phone had been a parting gift. *A reminder that you're not alone,* Annabel had said when she'd hugged Pam goodbye. Given how early it was on the west coast, Annabel was probably just now getting out of bed for her morning run before work.

"D'you make it through the night?" Annabel asked without preamble. "I've been worrying about you ever since you called last night. That was a hell of a lot dropped on you."

"Tell me about it." Pam felt like some hapless cartoon character with a big hole through her middle where a cannonball had been fired. "But, yeah, I made it through. Booze-free."

One might assume that was a perk of being near broke—not having the funds to fall off the wagon—but there had been a few years in her past when she simply would have undone a couple of top buttons, made her way to Wade's Watering Hole and struck up a conversation until some guy bought her a drink or two. Or six. She fought back a ripple of shame with the reminder that she'd been sober eight months and counting. She clenched trembling fingers into a fist. *Never again.*

"I'm a little shaky right now," Pam admitted, "but that's from lack of sleep."

"And the announcement that your mother is dead," Annabel said with brutal honestly. "*And* the news that your ex-husband and child are somewhere in the vicinity. Don't downplay what you're going through. You have a right to be angry and upset and conflicted."

"I'm not in denial, I'm just numb." Plus she was too exhausted to muster the energy for hysterics. She'd driven so far over the last few days, fueled by caffeine and a kind of grim eagerness. Having made the decision to confront Mae, she'd wanted to get it over with and, whatever happened between them, move on from there a healthier person. "I haven't had much rest lately."

"I won't keep you then," Annabel said. "When were you planning to see your aunt and uncle?"

"I'm going to call them after lunch, find out if they're back yet." She wondered nervously what kind of reception she'd get from her only remaining family. *Not your* only *family.*

Yes, they were, she argued with herself. Pam had given up any right to claim Faith years ago—probably the most responsible thing she'd ever done. Even at eighteen she'd realized what a train wreck of a mother she would be.

"If you're not going to track them down until after lunch, you still have a couple of hours to catch some z's." Annabel was half drill sergeant, half big sister. She was constantly admonishing Pam to eat, sleep and generally take better care of herself.

Rest, however, didn't seem to be in the cards. No sooner had Pam disconnected the call than there was a knock at her bedroom door. Surely it wasn't time to check out already?

"Coming, Trudy." As she shuffled to the door, Pam spared a second's thought for her attire. She wasn't exactly dressed for the day. Braless and bottomless except for a pair of bikini briefs, she wore a thin cotton T-shirt that was so oversized the hem fell halfway to her knees. Oh, well. The basics were covered. Cantankerous though she may be, Trudy didn't seem like the type of person who shocked easily.

Pam swung the door open, her greeting to the landlady dying unspoken on her lips. A fuse overloaded in her brain. She thought she could actually smell something burning as her mental processes short-circuited. Her mouth fell open, and an unintelligible squeak escaped. She glanced up—was it possible he'd gotten even taller?—into Nick Shepard's piercing blue eyes; they used to look to her like a tropical lagoon, all the faraway paradises she longed to visit. Now they looked like Judgment Day.

She couldn't have been any more startled and horrified if her mother's ghost had appeared at her door. "Y-you can't be here."

His lips twisted into a cruel line she couldn't

reconcile with the boy who'd loved her. "You seem confused about which one of us doesn't belong here, Pamela Jo."

"I meant, no, um, gentleman callers. Trudy's rule. And it's Pam." Hearing him say the name she used to go by brought back a flood of memories—the kind that required an ark if you were to have any chance at survival.

"What the hell are you doing in Mimosa, *Pam?*" The sneering tone made her think that even after all her years of resenting Mae, she was still just bush league when it came to anger. Here was a pro.

She swallowed, fighting the urge to huddle into herself for protection. Right now, his glinting, accusatory gaze was locked on hers. She was afraid that if she crossed her arms over her chest, she might draw his attention to the fact that she was clad only in a T-shirt. She doubted he cared what she was—or wasn't—wearing, but she felt painfully exposed already. "I came to town to talk to my mother."

Surprise momentarily softened his expression. Blinking, he rocked back on his heels, hands hooked in the pockets of his jeans. "You came to visit Mae? Voluntarily?" A rhetorical question since he didn't give her time to answer or explain. Cloaked once again in cold hostility, he asked, "You do know you're too late?"

"I know." She registered the taste of blood and realized she'd bitten her bottom lip. Hard. "I know I'm too late. I know I can't…fix anything." A fragment of the usual prayer tolled in her head like mournful bells. *The serenity to accept what I cannot change.* Today, there was no comfort in the phrase, only bleak finality.

She gripped the edge of the door, steeling herself. A stronger person—one whose inner core hadn't been mindlessly shrieking *ohGod-ohGod* ever since she'd seen Nick's face—would pull herself together and try to turn this disaster into an opportunity. If she couldn't make amends for what she'd put him through, she could at least ease his mind, assure him she didn't have any nefarious agenda. *Grant me the courage.* "Look. Nick."

He flinched, no less affected than she'd been when he said her name.

"I'm not staying. I have to see my aunt and uncle today, but then I'll be moving on." That's all she'd wanted for years, to be able to move forward, instead of uselessly spinning her wheels and looping in the same self-destructive cycle. She needed to let go of her past and build a new life with healthy habits and achievable, short-term goals.

Right now, her most pressing goal was to survive this conversation.

"I see." Finally he broke eye contact, and Pam's lungs remembered how to expand.

She took a much needed breath, assuming he would go now.

But instead he took a challenging half step toward her, his voice a blade. "So your plan is to run away. Again."

With the element of surprise on his side, Nick Shepard had believed he was prepared to see her—until she'd opened the door. Shards of the past cut into him like slivers into the tender spot of a foot, an excruciatingly sharp wound that doesn't even start bleeding immediately, as if the skin is still trying to process what the hell just happened. Dozens of disjointed memories sliced at him, most involving Pamela Jo, some more recent—such as a conversation he'd had with his daughter about impulse control and making good choices.

Where had his impulse control been just now? What on earth had possessed him to blurt that jab about her running away? It was what he *wanted,* for her to get as far away from Mimosa as geographically possible and never return. But he'd made it sound almost as if…he were daring her to stay.

She looked as perplexed as he felt, her eyes narrowed in confusion.

Faith had her mother's eyes, but that meant something different on any given day, the changeable hazel reflecting various amounts of gold, brown or green depending on her mood and what she wore.

For instance, Pamela Jo's eyes were a particularly vivid green because of that damn T-shirt. He'd been battling throughout their conversation to somehow *un*-notice that she was braless beneath that flimsy material. She was almost too thin, but certain curves had not diminished with time. And what kind of woman answered the door with no pants? He stubbornly ignored the fantasies he used to harbor about this exact woman opening doors to him wearing even less.

That had been a different reality. He was a single father now, not a horny teenager.

"So are you angry that I'm here," she asked cautiously, "or angry because I'm leaving?"

Both. Neither.

If someone had broached the subject of Pamela Jo two days ago, before he'd learned she was in town, he would have said his long dormant anger had faded away. She no longer meant anything to him; so long as he was with his daughter, everything had worked out for the best. The swell of fury he'd experienced when Pamela Jo had met his gaze had knocked him off balance.

He shoved a hand through his hair. "I didn't want you here—*don't* want you here—but it's a small town. There's a chance that…" It was more difficult than he could have imagined to say their daughter's name, as if a superstitious part of him worried that by mentioning Faith, he was somehow putting her at risk. "People know you're in Mimosa, and people gossip. It's likely that Faith will find out you're here, and I don't know how she'll react."

Pamela Jo's eyes were wide. "I wouldn't have… I thought you… Damn it, why aren't you in North Carolina?"

As if he owed her any explanations? Like hell. Still, the words tumbled out. "I moved here after the divorce. My wife betrayed me," he said with deceptive matter-of-factness. "Story of my life."

"Nick, I—"

He held up his hand. "Don't you dare apologize." There was no way that all they'd shared, and ultimately hadn't shared, could be encapsulated in a trite *I'm sorry.*

Her chin lifted, that one action suddenly making her look like the lover he'd once known, instead of a pretty stranger with short hair and eyes too like his daughter's. On closer inspection, he saw that there were shadowed crescents beneath Pamela Jo's eyes, yet another detail he didn't particularly want to see.

"My condolences on your mother's passing," he said brusquely. He didn't care overly much about what Pamela Jo was going through, but he needed a return to civil conversation. To normalcy.

She hesitated only briefly before reverting to their previous topic, the one that made him the most uneasy. "You think my passing through will hurt Faith?"

"It might raise some questions, some conflicted feelings, but she and I will deal with them. I shouldn't have brought that up." He was Faith's family, the one constant in her life—as she'd been in his since she was born—and he would find a way to give her whatever assurances she needed. Despite his resolve, however, he couldn't help thinking about all their recent arguing. Was his daughter pulling away from him? *I won't let that happen.*

But standing in front of Pamela Jo, who looked so much like their daughter and had once ripped his heart out by walking away from him, magnified his uneasiness.

Coming here had been a mistake. "Don't worry about us. Faith and I will be fine," he insisted. "I won't bother you again. Conclude whatever business you have here, and have a nice life."

With one final nod, he spun on his heels and walked toward the staircase. He regretted his earlier taunt more than ever. Because, despite his calm manner and deliberately slowed stride, it felt very much as if he were the one running away.

Chapter Four

Nick's retreat was almost as unexpected as his arrival. *That's it?* Pam stared out into the empty hall, knowing she should be relieved but feeling strangely bemused. Considering what he must have gone through after she'd left him and their infant daughter without a word of warning, he was entitled to be angry, enraged even.

So it seemed almost…anticlimactic that he'd suddenly calmed down, told her to have a nice life and left. Granted, there'd been an unmistakably implied "and stay the hell away from us" at the end of his farewell, but that was still far gentler than she'd deserved. She shut the door, shaking her head at her irrational discontent. *What, did you* want *him to scream at you?*

Maybe. It might have been cathartic for him to get it off his chest, they might have achieved some measure of closure. She sank into a sitting position against the wall, too drained from their encounter to walk back to the bed. Instead of feeling they'd reached any resolution, now she worried about what he'd let slip before backpedaling. Would her being here, no matter how temporarily, have negative repercussions for Faith? That Pam hadn't expected her daughter to be anywhere near Mimosa when she'd planned this trip didn't stop a small kernel of guilt from forming.

But trying to second-guess the emotional reaction of a near-teenager she didn't know was impossible. Pam's mind stumbled back to Nick, someone she'd once known intimately. It had been amazing how quickly he'd reined in his emotions today. In his younger years, he'd been very direct. Whether he'd been on the football field or romancing her, he'd always been clear about what he wanted and let others know that he would pursue his goals diligently. The only times she'd ever seen him censor himself had been during their brief, ultimately doomed, marriage, when they'd lived with his parents.

Truth be told, he'd reminded Pam a little of his parents just now. Polite, by way of the Arctic Circle.

As a teen, Pam had liked to believe she was tough, impossible to intimidate. After all, she'd grown up alone in a house with a temperamental alcoholic. But she'd been scared to death of Gwendolyn Shepard. Instead of raging when she'd learned about the pregnancy—Mae's diatribe had blurred in Pam's memory, but "ungrateful whore" had been the recurring theme—Nick's mother had been icy calm.

Well, then, I suppose that's that. Welcome to the family.... Naturally you'll be wearing ivory for the wedding instead of white.

Prior to announcing that his girlfriend was pregnant, Nick had never let his parents down. He'd been the slightly spoiled baby of the family who spent his short marriage trying to win back parental approval. The diplomatic balancing act couldn't have been easy on him, but, at the time, all Pam had been able to see was the way he didn't stand up for her. When she'd complained to him about it, he'd insisted she had to be patient with his parents, that they'd adjust in time. Meanwhile, she'd felt as if the entire Shepard family had ganged up on her—

including the newest Shepard, a baby girl who shrieked all the time.

Pam's recollections of those awful postpartum months were hazy, but she remembered Faith crying constantly, as if the infant had been channeling her mother's confusion and misery. *She was better off without me.*

"Miz Wilson! You up there?" Trudy's footsteps sounded on the stairs, nearly as loud as her strident voice. A frail old lady, Trudy was not.

"Yes, ma'am," Pam called back, summoning the energy to stand. *Get back on your feet.* It was a life lesson it seemed she was always learning. Some day, she vowed, all of this would be behind her and she truly would be able to stand on her own, without daily calls to Annabel. Maybe—in the distant future—Pam would even be stable enough to be there for others, help them regain their balance.

Some day. Pam opened the door to her room, checking the impulse to ask Trudy why she'd let Nick up here? "Good morning. You're the second surprise visitor I've had today."

Trudy's snowy brows lifted. "And this is how you greet visitors? Where are your clothes, girl? Day's half over."

"I drove to Mississippi from California. I had some sleep to catch up on."

"You just be sure and catch up on your sleep alone." Trudy craned her head, scrutinizing the bedroom. "That Nick Shepard isn't still up here, is he? He promised he'd take only a few minutes of your time and that he needed to see you immediately because it was a family emergency." She snorted. "I suppose you're gonna try to tell me you two are cousins?"

"No, ma'am." Given how bleak her morning had been so far, Pam couldn't help the small, perverse moment of humor she took in startling Trudy as she revealed, "He's my ex-husband."

Trudy's mouth fell open, but she recovered quickly. "You're the gal who cheated on him in North Carolina?"

So it had been an affair? He'd implied as much, but Lord knows, there were lots of different ways to betray a loved one. Pam couldn't imagine any woman throwing away marriage to Nick. She herself wouldn't have left him if it had been just the two of them. He'd made her feel safe in a way no one else ever had, before or since. Plus, he was a wickedly good kisser, although, now that she'd seen him, that memory was uncomfortable. Nick was no longer abstract nostalgia but a living, breathing, solidly male part of her present. There'd been such heat coming off of him that Pam fancied a red-and-yellow outline of his body might still be visible if you were looking through one of those thermal scanners they used in movies.

"I'm not the one from North Carolina," she said. "And I didn't cheat on him."

"Just how many wives does this guy have?"

"Only two that I know of." She recalled his saying he'd moved back to Mimosa "after the divorce."

Reassured that Nick wasn't a bigamist, Trudy turned her disapproval back to Pam. "And I suppose you think you can do better than him?"

Pam smiled sadly. "Not really." She'd feared more than once that Nick Shepard would be the best thing that ever happened to her. "But that doesn't mean I get to stop living, just because the good old days are behind me. Right?"

Trudy pursed her lips. "I wouldn't know. I'm smack in the middle of my prime."

Pam's first sip of god awful tea in her aunt's antique-filled living room dredged up a long buried memory.

"Mom, do I have to drink it?" Even as a first-grader, Pam had been appalled by the idea of unsweetened tea. Iced tea in the south was syn-

onymous with generous amounts of sugar. The bitter flavor of the special herbal blend aside, she'd also been alarmed by the long list of "beneficial" ingredients her aunt had recited. *"She said there were geckos in this."*

Mae had looked blank for a second, then laughed, smiling at her daughter with amused affection. *"Ginkgo, Pammy Jo. Not gecko. Although lizards probably taste better."*

Now, decades later, Pam's fingers clenched around the glass. It seemed surreal that the frosted vintage set her aunt had used since the seventies was exactly the same when so much else had changed. "I can't believe she's dead."

Julia Danvers Calbert sniffed. "Then you're deluded. The way my sister drank and carried on, the mystery isn't that she's passed, it's that she lived so long."

"Julia!" The one-word rebuke from quiet Uncle Ed was unprecedented. It was clear just from the seating arrangements who reigned over conversation. While Julia sat as regally and straight-shouldered as a queen in a richly upholstered wing chair, Uncle Ed was wedged into a ridiculously dainty chair with a heart-shaped back and gilded gold legs. It looked very expensive and very uncomfortable.

"I'm only telling the truth," his wife protested. "And she's grown up enough to hear it. She's not little Pammy Jo anymore."

"Still…" Flushing a bright pink that shone through his salt-and-pepper beard, Ed gave his niece an apologetic smile. "Whatever her age, she's a woman who just lost her mama."

"Just?" Julia shot to her feet. "No, Mae died months ago, if you'll remember. And we had to deal with everything. Because this one—" her words illustrated by an accusing jab of the index finger "—was off gallivanting who knows where."

"California," Pam declared reflexively.

"Exactly!" Julia nodded, repeating the word with some venom. "*California.* I suppose you'll content yourself with putting a few flowers on your mother's grave and then head right back to the Sunshine State with little thought for the rest of us?"

Pam opened her mouth to inform her aunt that the Sunshine State was actually Florida, but bit her tongue. She'd never seen Julia, the proper, understated Danvers sister, quite so worked up before and didn't want to add fuel to the fire. Pam never would have said that her mother and aunt were close—indeed, they seemed to hold a mutual contempt for each other's lifestyles— but Julia's hands were trembling and she blinked as if determined to keep tears at bay. Was she grieving Mae's death?

"I won't be returning to California," Pam said. She doubted she could scrape together the gas money to get as far as Alabama, much less the west coast. "I don't honestly know what my plans are from here, but—"

"You don't have a job you need to get back to, then? A husband waiting for you?" Julia's voice had softened, more weary resignation than censure.

"No, ma'am."

Her aunt, like most normal people, might view the lack of a family and a career as failure. But what Pam *did* have waiting for her if she chose to return were weekly meetings and a sponsor. Which meant there was at least a chance for some kind of eventual success; that was more than she'd been able to say in a long time.

"I should bring out the rest of the tea," Julia announced abruptly. Never mind that all three of their glasses were still full.

Pam shot a questioning look at her uncle. Since when was Julia so high-strung? When he said nothing to fill the ensuing silence, she prompted, "Is Aunt Julia okay?"

"The circumstances have been hard on her,"

Ed answered, so quietly that Pam strained her ears to follow his words. "Losing her sister, to some extent. But mostly…losing you."

"Me?" Pam had grown up with the vague sense that Julia didn't like her. Julia had never seemed to much like anyone.

"There were things between your mama and your aunt." He stopped himself, shooting a guilty look toward the kitchen. "If Julia was ever hard on you, it's because she wanted better for you. She loves you. You know how she always finishes her Christmas shopping so early? That fall, when you left town, I found her in our room, crying over a package with your name on it. It's still in her closet. She's refused to donate it to charity, even though we didn't know if you were ever coming back. Or if you were even alive."

Tendrils of guilt curled through Pam like smoke, making it difficult to breathe. After her reckless flight from Mimosa, she'd spent sleepless nights alternately regretting the way she'd left Nick and hatefully hoping that her mother was worried sick. It had genuinely never occurred to her that her sudden absence might hurt Julia and Ed. Even with the picture he painted, Pam still couldn't imagine her starchy aunt shedding tears. *I wasn't worth them.*

"Uncle Ed, I'm…"

"You're what?" Julia asked from the doorway, her expression suspicious. "Sorry to interrupt, I just couldn't contain my curiosity. What have the two of you been discussing? Pam's exciting life beyond Mimosa?"

Exciting was one word for it. Pam reached for the ends of her hair, a nervous girlhood habit. She had a moment's disorientation before she remembered that she'd hacked a good six inches off of it last year and had been keeping it short ever since. She rose. "Can I help you with that tray, Aunt Julia?"

A pitcher of tea sat between a plate of muffins and—*hallelujah*—a china bowl of sugar.

"I think not," her aunt said. "This pitcher is vintage. Everyone knows fatigue makes people unsteady, and you look like you haven't had a full night's sleep in a month of Sundays. You'll stay with us tonight, not out there at Trudy's."

It took Pam a moment to process the imperious decree as an invitation. "Thank you. It's kind of you to offer."

"Well, we're kin." Julia sniffed. "Not that you could tell from the number of messages and letters we've had from you over the years."

Now, beneath the criticism, Pam heard the decade plus of worry. "I'm so sorry I never let you know where I was." Sorry for all of their sakes. If she'd allowed herself that familial anchor, would she have turned to them for help before she hit rock bottom?

Probably not. Hitting rock bottom was why she'd finally admitted she needed help.

"We knew you were in Tennessee, of course," her uncle offered with exaggerated joviality. "It was something else, seeing you on television!"

"Oh." Pam had only been on a regional cable channel, and she'd never been entirely sure whether her show was available this far out. "Thank you. I went to California after that. Guess I was hoping to do even more television, but it didn't pan out."

She'd first been "discovered" playing guitar and singing in a Tennessee bar. All those juvenile dreams she and Nick used to spin—about her eventual fame, and his leading an NFL team to the Super Bowl, where she would *naturally* sing at halftime—had kept her afloat when she was alone and scared out of her mind. Despite a small-time talent agent's attempts, she'd never progressed beyond the periphery of the music industry. In the fading heyday of music videos, she'd briefly held a job as a video jockey, hosting a weekly country music countdown and reading entertainment-news bulletins.

But she'd yearned to find validation through stardom and quickly grew unhappy reporting on other people's fame. So she quit a perfectly good job—the best one she'd ever had, really—to go with her loser boyfriend of the time to California. What followed had been a downward spiral of bad decisions and bad boyfriends.

Ironic. Pam remembered clearly the day she'd looked into her infant daughter's squalling face and panicked at the flare of resentment that pierced her postpartum numbness. In that moment, Pam had realized how easily she could become like her own mother—a former prom queen who took her disappointment in life out on her kid and anesthetized herself with booze and men. So Pam had fled, wanting more for herself and more for baby Faith. *I ran like hell, all the way to the opposite coast. Where I promptly turned into Mae.*

The silver lining was that she hadn't dragged her daughter down with her.

"You and your mother," Julia chided, unknowingly echoing Pam's thoughts. "Always so ambitious, always wanting more."

"Like what?" Pam asked. "I never heard Mae mention wanting to be an actress." Pam had grown up with the sense that her mother was deeply unhappy without ever having any idea what it would take to fix that.

"She wanted to be adored. Everyone was so surprised when beautiful, outgoing Mae married your father, who, let's face it, was a shy, awkward man. But I know what the attraction was—that mile-high pedestal he had her on. He worshipped her like a goddess, and she treated him like... Well, he snapped after just a year and ran off with a clerk from the bookstore. A man needs to be nurtured! He can't stay married to a woman who intimidates him."

Pam wondered absently if Julia had become a more nurturing wife over the past decade; it wasn't how Pam remembered her aunt and uncle's relationship. Then again, what did Pam know? She'd always had the impression that her father had left because of *her,* because he wasn't sure he was ready to be a father and because his physical interest in Mae had waned during her pregnancy.

"I'll never be beautiful again," Mae had complained one summer, meeting her young daughter's eyes in a dressing room mirror. *"Pretty, sure, but I was stunning once. You ruined that. See these stretch marks? I got huge with you. No wonder your daddy left us."*

To Pam, *daddy* had seemed as exotic and

nonsensical as *unicorn*. Her biological father had never been more than the name on her birth certificate and monthly checks. Who knew what his side of the story sounded like? In her first year after leaving Mimosa, she'd suffered periodic anxiety attacks, waking in the middle of the night, worrying what Nick would tell their daughter about her own absent parent. For herself, Pam didn't care—she deserved anything he had to say about her—but she'd prayed he was careful with the girl's feelings, that Faith would never blame herself.

Faith. The name came more naturally to mind after this morning's talk with Nick. For years Pam had continued to think of their daughter as "the baby," long after she'd no doubt been enrolled in school.

"Speaking of ex-husbands," Pam began hesitantly, "do either of you see Nick Shepard much? I understand he'd moved away but is back in town now."

Julia and Ed exchanged a glance that made Pam ache inside. For all that Julia could be domineering and Ed could be oblivious, they clearly shared a bond. An entire conversation seemed to pass between them in a single moment of crystalline silence.

"That's what we heard, too," Julia said. "But, no. We…stay out of his way."

"Right after you left, he used to come by," Ed added. "A lot. He was convinced we knew where you were. Or that you'd contact us. After a few months, he realized we were as in the dark as he was."

Pam winced. "I'm sorry. For any worry I put you through. I didn't—I'm sorry."

"It's done now," Julia said decisively. "Maybe you could start fresh, now that your mama left you the house. Move back to Mimosa. Your uncle might even be able to hire you on part-time at the furniture showroom—"

"Absolutely not." Once the words were out, Pam regretted shooting down her aunt so quickly. Maybe she should have pretended to consider settling here for a millisecond, to spare Julia's feelings.

But really? Move back to emotional ground zero? No. She couldn't quite wrap her mind around doing that even if Nick and Faith hadn't been in Mississippi. With them here, it was impossible. Recalling the furious intensity in Nick's blue eyes, she could just imagine the fit he'd throw if she announced she was staying. Pam shivered.

"I don't know exactly what my plans for the

future are," she reiterated gently. "But I can't see myself in Mimosa long-term. How can I start fresh by going back? I want to stay for a little while—at the house, if I become an imposition here—and I want to keep in touch with the two of you when I go. But I will be moving on." That part was imperative.

Uncle Ed cleared his throat. "We understand," he said, overtop of his wife's entreaties. "The important thing is, you're here now."

After a moment, Julia nodded her reluctant agreement. "I'll start on dinner in a few hours. A big dinner! You're too scrawny. In the meantime, have some muffins. And drink your tea—it's good for you."

Pam eyed the glass in her hand. *Beverage penance.* Sure, why not? She took a big drink, meeting her beaming aunt's gaze. Bleah. Yet considering where Pam was, other things coming her way would likely be much harder to swallow.

Chapter Five

"Pssst, Faith!"

Faith Shepard shot her best friend a warning glance. Even though both girls were finished with their pop quizzes, Morgan knew what a stickler Mrs. Branch was about talking in class. After yesterday, Faith was in enough trouble at home without her lit teacher sending a disciplinary note. Faith used to think of her dad as one of her best friends—not that she would ever say something so dorky out loud. In the last year, though…

She didn't know what was going on exactly, but lately it didn't take much for her previously cool dad to freak out. Maybe it was the divorce. Or Grandma Gwendolyn always harping on him.

"I have to talk to you," Morgan whispered urgently. She always sounded urgent.

Keeping her eyes on the teacher's desk, where Mrs. Branch had started grading, Faith asked out of the corner of her mouth, "About Kyle?" The way Morgan rhapsodized, you would think Kyle Gunn was Robert Pattinson's hot younger brother.

Morgan shook her head slowly, also keeping her gaze forward. When she spoke again, her lips barely moved. The two girls could totally do their own ventriloquism act on one of those talent search shows. "No. About *you*."

What? Faith abandoned their eyes-front subterfuge, whipping her head in Morgan's direction. What did her friend know? Did it have to do with the strange murmurings in the cafeteria today when Faith passed, the way that hag Arianne had snickered this morning?

"After class," Faith whispered, hardly caring anymore if they were caught. "My house."

Nick came home early for two reasons. The first was, he'd been thinking about his daughter all day and wanted to be there for her—even though he doubted she'd welcome his presence.

Less than twenty-four hours ago, he'd grounded her, which meant he was destined to be persona non grata for a few sulky days.

The other reason he came home was much simpler. He oversaw a construction crew. And men who were distracted shouldn't be around power tools and huge pieces of motorized equipment.

"Faith?" He walked through the back door, entering the kitchen and calling out her name. Based on the past few times they'd clashed, she would be holed up in her room, blasting some sort of music guaranteed to annoy anyone over the age of twenty-five, pretending not to hear him.

So it came as a surprise when she met him at the edge of the kitchen tile, hands on her slim hips, glaring at him through exceedingly red eyes. The eyes combined with her sniffling made it clear she'd just finished a crying jag.

"Faith? What is it, honey?" Stupid question, when he already knew the answer. The coincidence was too great. But on the one-percent chance that this wasn't about Pamela Jo Wilson, he held his breath and waited for his daughter's reply.

"Is it true? Is my mom in town?"

Nick sucked in a breath, wondering for the

millionth time when this parenting gig was going to get easier. That entire first year, when Faith had been so tiny and fragile, he'd been scared witless. He'd told himself that when she was bigger, stronger, it wouldn't be so excruciating. But then there'd come the day when he'd had to put her on the bus to kindergarten, and it had been like taking shrapnel in the chest. Which had been nothing compared to the first time she told him she liked a boy. And now...

"It's true."

She deflated, arms dropping, shoulders hunching. "I was hoping you didn't know. I thought, no way would he keep something like this from me. I found out from *Morgan,* Dad. You don't even like Morgan! Half the school knew before me. Or figured, anyway. Someone's mom knew that you and this chick used to be a thing, so people were wondering... Do you know how squicked I was to hear that people were talking about my parents' sex—"

"Please stop." Nick flinched, hoping he'd never hear his daughter use the word *sex* again. While he wasn't sure what the exact definition of *squick* was, he felt confident that he was right there with her. "If it makes you feel better, I haven't known long, either. And it's why I came home early today. Why don't we sit in the living room?" This wasn't going to be a simple conversation, suited to a few minutes of standing in a doorway.

"Okay." But instead of turning around, she marched further into the kitchen toward the refrigerator. She pulled out a gallon of mint-chocolate-chip ice cream, then went to the utensil drawer, shooting him a defiant look as she withdrew a spoon.

"Make it two," he told her. They could have ice cream for dinner and, if she was still hungry later, he'd make her salad for dessert.

They sat together on the couch, each digging into the tub while they collected their thoughts.

"Where do you want me to start?" Nick asked her.

"When I was born. You told me that you weren't married long because you wanted different things."

"That's right." *I wanted you, and she didn't.* He and Pamela Jo had both been alarmed to discover she was pregnant, but they'd married anyway. Nick had loved her, truly believed they were destined to be together. They'd even been eager to have a baby, in that clueless teenage way, with no idea of what parenting really entailed. Though it hadn't been easy—his trying to take community college classes while Pamela Jo read pregnancy books and tried to cope with his mother day after day—he'd thought they'd make it.

Until the baby came. Pam's personality had undergone a radical change. Worse than that, it was as if her personality had faded away. She'd shut him out when he'd tried to talk to her, and his mother had downplayed his fears, insisting that Pam was jealous of the baby and competing for Nick's attention with her listless "act."

Faith stabbed her spoon into the already softening ice cream. "You said she wanted more than life in Mimosa. Even if it was a jerky thing to leave her daughter, I guess I can understand her not wanting to be *here.* I miss Charlotte," she admitted with a sigh.

Had he done the wrong thing, moving them back here instead of staying in North Carolina? He certainly hadn't anticipated *this* when he made the decision.

"But here's what I don't get, Dad. I never really thought about it until Morgan was asking me questions, but if my mother wanted to leave Mimosa, why didn't you go with her? Why didn't the three of us go be a family somewhere else?"

Because she never gave me a choice. Never gave us a chance. "Honey, you know that sometimes marriages just don't work out. Like me and Jenna."

"That bombed because she had a guy on the side," Faith said flatly. She was unlikely to ever forgive her stepmother, which was a shame. Jenna was probably the closest Faith would ever come to a mom. "No mystery there."

"The truth was, Pamela Jo—your mother— and I were very, very young when we got married. Too young. Most people who get together as teenagers don't last forever."

Faith mulled this over. "All right," she said finally, once more the logical, reasonable daughter he knew and not the stranger who'd been breaking rules and picking fights with him lately.

Nick exhaled with relief. *I should have known.* Faith was a good kid. When you got right down to it, he'd been damned lucky. Maybe his visit to Pamela Jo this morning had been an overreaction. He dug his spoon into the ice cream with renewed appetite.

"Dad?"

He looked up with an expectant smile. "Yeah?"

"I want to meet her."

"Pamela Jo!" Julia's voice carried easily from the front of the house to the kitchen. "You have company."

Pam was startled enough that she almost dropped the Jewel Tea dinner plate in her hand, one of her aunt's Autumn Leaf collection. She corrected at the last moment, so that the dish slid harmlessly into the warm waiting suds. "Y-you're sure?" Her pulse doubled and she struggled to control it.

What were the odds of Nick Shepard tracking her down twice in one day? She felt ridiculous even considering it. The man wanted nothing to do with her.

"PJ the VJ!" There was an excited—and thankfully very female—squeal of excitement from the foyer, then the clatter of high-heeled footsteps across Julia's hardwood floors. A round brunette came into view. Petite but very curvy, she'd seemingly fashioned her entire look from circles: glossy curls, black hoop earrings that nearly brushed her shoulders and a rainbow of polka dots covering her black sundress. "Ohmigod, I can't believe it's really you! I mean, my sister told me. But I had to see for myself."

Unlike with Nick, whom Pam would probably recognize in every fiber of her being even if fifty years had passed, it took a split second to place this person from her past. "Dawn?"

The brunette grinned. "In the flesh."

Tears pricked Pam's eyes, startling her. In

the past twenty-four hours, she'd weathered the news that her mother had died and that Nick Shepard lived just around the corner. So why should seeing an old friend elicit the waterworks? "You look good. Really good."

Although Dawn Lewin might be plumper than was strictly fashionable, she'd always been good with hair and makeup. She'd fixed Pam's hair before countless choir solos and high school dances. In the years since Pam had seen her last, her friend appeared to have outgrown a certain girlish anxiousness. As a teen, Dawn had been cute but insecure; now she exuded a subtle confidence that magnified her charm. Pam felt a twinge of envy. Her own confidence could use a boost these days.

"You look like you've been on some kind of killer diet," Dawn countered. "I am *never* gonna fit into jeans that skinny. But you have split ends," she added critically. "You're not so thin that I'll break you if I hug you?"

Pam shook her head, stepping forward to meet the other woman halfway. Dawn smelled like chocolate and expensive hair care products and her hug was more comforting than Pam could have imagined. She retreated quickly, embarrassed.

"I didn't realize how much I needed a hug.

Thank you. I just found out about my mother yesterday," she said by way of awkward explanation.

Dawn clucked her tongue sympathetically. "I thought of you when she passed. Would have sent a card if I'd had any idea where you were. My sister and I used to watch you religiously when you were on that country music show. Then you disappeared and I told her, one of these days, we're gonna go to the Mimosa Cineplex and she's gonna be smiling at us from the big screen."

Pam managed not to roll her eyes in self-derision. She was about the furthest thing possible from a movie star. "Hardly, but thanks for believing in me. Wait, your sister—*that's* who I saw at Granny K's, your little sister, Summer?" The statuesque twentysomething who'd been staring at her was the erstwhile pig-tailed kid who used to beg Pam and Dawn to paint her nails and include her on their gossip? Pam felt like Rip Van Winkle, waking to find the entire world had changed.

"Not so little now, is she?" Dawn burbled with laughter. "I have to wear three-inch heels just to look her in the eye."

From the kitchen doorway, Julia delicately cleared her throat. "Pamela Jo?"

"Yes, ma'am?" Pam had given up telling

her aunt that she didn't go by her full name anymore—she doubted the woman would change a lifelong habit. But being called Pamela Jo didn't bother her here the way it had when Nick used it this morning. She had too many memories of his saying her name. The day he'd first told her he'd loved her, the many times they'd made love, the infrequent times they'd argued, the day their daughter was born.

"Don't you want to offer your guest a place to sit and be comfortable?" Julia prompted. "Maybe get her some tea?"

Heck, no. Pam liked Dawn way too much to inflict The Tea upon her. Instead, she smiled at her old friend. "Want to sit on the porch and catch up?" There was a slight breeze outside and the sun had set enough for the temperature to dip below baking.

"Perfect! I want to hear about everything you've been up to since you left," Dawn enthused as they headed for the front door.

"Um…not much to tell, really. You witnessed the pinnacle of my 'fame.'" She made air quotes with her fingers, shaking her head at the memory of PJ the VJ. She settled into one of the creaky rockers on the porch, and Dawn sat on the padded striped bench across from her. "After the video jockey gig, I tried a few things that didn't really work out. But tell me all about you! Are you even still Dawn Lewin, or is it Mrs. Some-Lucky-Guy now?"

Dawn's cheeks grew rosy. "Not yet, but I'm hoping he'll pop the question next month. I've been dropping hints that an engagement ring would be a very nice birthday present. You don't know him—Jerry Price. He moved here about five years ago."

Pam nodded politely, although it was still an adjustment to consider Mimosa a place people would move *to;* for her, the town had always been something to escape. Of course, now that she'd actually seen Nashville and Los Angeles and myriad places in between, she had to admit some of the destinations she used to dream of weren't all they were cracked up to be. And she'd seriously missed the food at Granny K's.

Leaning forward on the bench, Dawn asked, "What about you? Got a special man in your life?" She bit the inside of her cheek. "I feel silly bringing this up—it was all so long ago, you probably don't even think about him these days—but you do know Nick Shepard is in town? If I were you, it's the kind of thing I'd want a friend to tell me. That way you can run out for groceries in cute shoes and lipstick. Just in case. I mean, because you're over an ex doesn't mean you want to bump into him on laundry day when the closest you've come to a hairstyle is a ball cap. Am I right?"

"Absolutely spot-on." She considered sharing with Dawn her embarrassing encounter from that morning. Joking with the cheerful brunette about it might even make it seem funny. But Pam found the words wouldn't quite come. It was still too fresh.

Dawn twined a strand of her dark hair around a finger, looking tentative. "We were friends a long time, so I hope this won't seem like stabbing you in the back. But I sort of made a play for Nick myself. You'd been gone for months, and no one knew if you'd be back, so…"

"You don't owe me any apology for that!" Pam assured her friend. *If I'd wanted him, I should have kept him.* Except it had never been about not wanting Nick. It was just the rest of the package—his unwelcoming parents, this suffocating town. The baby. "I left. Nick was completely available."

And based on what he'd said that morning, he was again.

"Well, it's not like anything ever happened anyway. We went out once or twice, but he had his hands full. I haven't even seen him since he moved back."

I have. An awkward silence descended.

Dawn nibbled at the bright lipstick on her lower lip. "If you're looking to meet a guy, Jerry has a few single friends."

"Thanks, but I'm not staying," Pam said quickly. Did she really seem so pathetic that someone might think her only prospects for a relationship would come from a total stranger? "I'll probably just be in town a few days." She'd use the time to try and forge a bond with her aunt and uncle and find a competent real estate agent to list Mae's—*her own*—house.

Was there a property version of selling a broken-down car for parts? Because Pam couldn't imagine anyone actually living in the neglected home she'd seen yesterday afternoon.

"Oh, right." Dawn smiled contritely. "I don't know why I'd think you were staying permanently." She stared out at the road in front of them, and Pam wondered if the woman was regretting her impromptu visit. *I hope not.* Dawn was the first person who'd seemed unequivocally delighted to see Pam, harboring no bitterness over her abrupt departure a lifetime ago.

A pickup truck rumbled down the street, and it wasn't until the vehicle had practically reached the Calberts' driveway that Pam read the logo printed on one of the cab doors. Bauer and

Shepard Construction. Her stomach clenched. She sat stock-still, unable to take her gaze off the impending doom.

Let it be a coincidence, she thought stupidly. But the truck rolled into the drive and, a heartbeat later, Nick Shepard emerged.

Dawn's breath caught. "Oh, my good Lord," she whispered. "That man got even better-looking over time."

On a completely objective level, Pam supposed her friend was right. But it was hard to appreciate the appeal of his long, lithe body, chiseled features and laser-bright eyes when he looked angry enough to do someone violence. *Specifically, this someone.*

He closed the space between them with powerful strides. Though he was still in jeans, he'd changed shirts since she'd seen him that morning. The white polo shirt he had on now emphasized his tan. He obviously spent a lot of time out in the sun. A random memory hit her, the two of them by a secluded, sun-dappled pond— her alternately fretting that someone might actually happen along and laughing that if she didn't put back on certain pieces of clothing, she could end up sunburned in vulnerable areas. She'd realized later that Faith had been conceived by that pond.

Suddenly Nick slowed his gait and conjured a smile. "Dawn Lewin, I didn't see you there. Been a while."

Dawn nodded like a bobble-headed doll, hand at her throat. "Sure has. But you don't look any older."

"I was just thinking the same about you," he said. "I hate to run you off, Dawn, but would you mind if—"

"Of course!" The accommodating brunette bounced out of her seat, grinning at Pam. "You and I can finish reminiscing some other time. Stop by C-3 before you leave town, and I'll do your hair for free. It just has to be after hours."

"C-3?" Pam repeated dumbly. *Like that gold robot in those movies?*

"Cut, Curl and Color. You remember the salon on Witherspoon Drive? The owner thought C-3 made us sound more modern and less like the place where Eugenia Ellsberry has been requesting the same blue rinse since 1978." This explanation came mostly over Dawn's shoulder as she hustled down the front porch steps. She disappeared into the little compact parked at the curb and was gone all too soon. Pam hadn't even had a chance to summon her aunt and uncle from inside the house as witnesses.

She gauged the leashed anger in Nick's rigid

posture and sighed. *Will people even know where to look for my body?* Dragging that pond might be a good start.

"We have to stop meeting like this," she drawled. It was stupid to bait him, but for the life of her, she couldn't think of what the right thing to say would be. "Did you come here because you realized you didn't yell at me nearly enough this morning?" Darn it, she'd known she got off too easily.

"No." He clenched and unclenched his hands. "I came here because my daughter asked me to."

Chapter Six

Nick took the porch stairs two at a time, reminding himself to keep his cool. For Faith's sake, this meeting needed to be productive. Besides, he knew what kind of lecture he would suffer through when he returned home and had to face his mother—might as well make sure this was worth it.

Pam had gone pale. Because of his unannounced appearance or because he'd mentioned their child?

"Faith heard that I'm in town," she concluded.

"Yeah. And she wants to meet you."

"That's not a good idea." She'd already started

shaking her head before he even finished the sentence. "You know it's not. My meeting her can't be what you want."

Hell no. Sitting there in jeans and a flowy, printed blouse with short sleeves and a square neckline, strands of her blond hair dancing in the breeze, Pam looked harmless enough. Cute, even. But he knew firsthand the kind of destructive force she could be. He'd held her, crying in his arms, on more than one occasion after her own mother had wreaked emotional destruction on her. He'd be damned if he would let Pam wound Faith like that, which was why he'd argued with his daughter for an hour. Eventually, though, his little girl had convinced him that never meeting Pam, never looking her in the eye, might actually hurt more in the long run than anything Pam could say to her. He'd reluctantly agreed to plead Faith's case, but he couldn't pretend he'd be completely broken up if Pam said no and bailed on them.

Again.

Nick sighed. "It's not about what I want. She's a young woman and she deserves a mother." He held up a hand, forestalling the obvious objections in Pam's eyes. "But she's never really going to have that. So the least you could do for her is to meet her, let her see who she comes from.

Maybe even give her a few answers. Is that really asking so much?"

Fear radiated from her, taking him aback. He'd fallen in love with an ambitious, bold girl. Even when he'd seen her cry, the tears had stemmed as much from frustration and anger as vulnerability. Yet from the moment the doctors had placed Faith in Pam's arms at the hospital, panic had become her default setting. Was the unnatural terror really so strong, almost thirteen years later, that she'd deny a blameless girl?

"I'm sure I'm coming across as some sort of evil villain," Pam huffed, her normally melodious drawl a harsh mutation of itself. "But I'm thinking of her more than me."

"Bullshit. Do not hide behind that. You don't know her well enough to know what's best for her."

Pam stood so abruptly that she flung the rocking chair into motion, pitching wildly back and forth. "I know what a train wreck I am! You haven't seen me in years, Nick. I could have a police record. Or split personalities!"

That would explain a lot.

"I can't be a mother," she insisted. "I can't even be a short-term role model."

"So be a cautionary tale," he snapped. "Whatever. You're placing too much importance on yourself. Let me bring her to you on neutral ground some afternoon before you leave Mimosa. Granny K's for milk shakes, half an hour, something like that. I don't think that in thirty minutes, you're going to warp a beautiful, intelligent young woman. She needs this closure. Don't be the what-if in her life, Pamela Jo. Don't be the hole inside her that she walks around with for years to come."

Unwillingly he remembered the first few days after Pam had left him. He hadn't even been truly upset for the initial seventy-two hours because he'd known her abandonment wasn't real. She'd had some postpartum hormone surge, he'd reasoned, temporary insanity. She'd be back. They belonged together. But when he'd realized… That cold, empty place she'd left in his life might have healed, but it had never completely warmed again. Not even when he married Jenna.

She'd called him on that when they fought over the affair, telling him that maybe deep down she'd wanted revenge because she felt as if he'd always kept part of himself from her.

Nick was never getting married again. *My taste in women sucks.*

"I'll think about it," Pam said. "But standing on my aunt's porch bullying me isn't going to get you the result you want any faster. Now, if you'll excuse me, I'm late for a meeting."

"Really?" He quirked an eyebrow. "You didn't seem to be in such a hurry to get rid of Dawn."

"Yeah, well, I didn't feel such a pressing need to go to a meeting when she was here, either."

He leaned in closer, studying her as intently as a forensics investigator seeking clues. She swallowed, shuffling back a little, although the rocker left her nowhere to go.

"You're serious," he decided. Despite her matter-of-fact tone, there was a barely banked urgency in her shifting eyes. "What kind of meeting?"

"AA. I scoped out times and places online, just in case." She gave a short bark of laughter. "Turns out the apple didn't fall far from the tree. I'm Mae's daughter through and through."

"Alcoholics Anonymous? But you never drank." The most he'd ever seen her imbibe was a wine cooler.

"I told you, Nick." Her voice softened, more apologetic than argumentative. "You don't know me."

"Not because I didn't want to." He locked gazes with her. "You took that choice away."

"It was the best thing for all of us."

Based on what, her woman's intuition? The

fact was, they'd never know. Maybe he and Pamela Jo and Faith could have been a happy family, once they'd found their footing, moved out of his parents' house. But she hadn't given them a chance.

"We'll have to agree to disagree," Nick said. He hadn't come here to debate the past. He just wanted to help Faith. "You should trust me, as the man who raised her, to have a good idea of what's best for my daughter now. She should meet you. Think about it?"

"Every waking second," she said grimly.

He took out his wallet and reached for his business cards. Holding one out to her, he said, "My number's on here. Let me know, whichever way you decide."

Her arms remained crossed over her chest. "I don't need that. It's a small town. I can find you."

Was she so determined to keep her distance from him and Faith that she couldn't even extend a hand? His temper sparked. "Just take the damn card, Pamela Jo."

"It's Pam."

He ground his teeth. "Take the card, Pam. Please."

With obvious reluctance, she complied, delicately grasping the very edge between her fingers. It stung more than it should have, the way she rejected him with every motion and mannerism. Why should he be surprised by her abhorrence to being around him or Faith? She'd made it clear in the letter she'd left on his nightstand years ago, the one that had granted him absolute, uncontested custody of the baby she didn't love.

Despite his promise to Faith, he teetered on the brink of just telling Pam to forget it, not to do them any favors.

But then she asked in a tiny voice, "Do you have a picture? Of how she looks now?"

The request startled him. "Yeah. Hang on." He once again retrieved his wallet, fumbling this time. An entire clear plastic section showcased Faith's maturation from a chubby-faced baby to the grinning honors student who would be dating boys and driving cars before he knew it. He pulled out her school photo from last spring. "This one's recent, only a few months old."

Pam swallowed. "She's beautiful."

She looks like her mother. Faith's hair was the same color as his, but she had Pam's features and build. "She has your smile." He wasn't sure why he was compelled to point that out, when surely Pam could see the resemblance for herself, or why he added, "And your voice."

Her gaze lifted. "She sings?"

"Like an angel." He thought about the lyrics to a Lady Gaga song Faith had been belting out in the car the previous week. "Angel might not be the right comparison."

Pam took the picture from him, studying it silently. He found himself holding his breath, as if unwilling to interrupt a private moment. Finally she nodded, handing the photo back. "Tell her I said yes. I'll meet her. But between you and me, I still think it's a mistake."

He told her what he always told his daughter. "Mistakes are how we learn."

"How did it go?" Gwendolyn Shepard asked from her chair at the kitchen table.

"Don't start, Mom."

"That well, hmm?"

Nick dropped into a seat, so weary he thought maybe he'd just sleep there tonight. "Thanks for coming over to keep an eye on Faith. Is she up in her room?"

"Getting ready to take a shower. We just finished eating." His mother's eyes narrowed. "A *real* dinner. Honestly, Nicholas, ice cream? She's a growing girl. You know how important nutrition is."

"I'll be nutritionally virtuous tomorrow," he

promised. "Today seemed like an ice-cream kind of day."

Above him, the second-story floor creaked. He heard the linen closet being opened and closed, then water rushing through the pipes. At least he knew he had a little while to regroup before Faith interrogated him, wanting all the details of his meeting with Pamela Jo.

"Let me fix you a plate," Gwendolyn suggested, scraping her chair back across the floor. "You look beat. I knew going to see that woman couldn't be a good idea."

"'That woman' is Faith's mother, and Faith is twelve years old. She's got a right to have a say in this. In most states, kids her age are allowed an opinion on who their custodial parent should be."

"Well, that's just ridiculous," Gwendolyn huffed. "Kids don't know what's good for them. That's why they have us."

He flashed a tired grin. "Us? So you finally trust me to know what's good for me?"

"Asks the man who served ice cream for dinner." Gwendolyn shook her head. But a moment later, when she was pulling clean plates out of the dishwasher and not looking at him, she added, "When your father died a couple of years ago, you proved to me what a solid adult you've become. I'm not sure I ever really thanked you for everything you did. I've always appreciated how you were there for me and Leigh."

"You're welcome," he said awkwardly. His father's affairs had all been in order, the details taken care of, so it wasn't as if Nick had been faced with any difficult decisions. It was more that his mom and sister had needed him to make phone calls they'd been too emotional to place.

But Jenna had later pointed to his dad's death as one of her examples of how estranged she and Nick were. She'd said that he didn't let her comfort him, that he'd never really trusted her with his whole heart. He wasn't sure whether she'd meant that part of his heart still belonged to his first wife, or if she'd been suggesting that Pamela Jo had somehow damaged him, making it impossible to fully love again. Either translation was annoying.

No matter. Jenna was hardly a credible source. She'd been trying to justify her adulterous actions; her words stemmed from defensive guilt, not reality.

He had to admit, though, that seeing Pamela Jo again had stirred up…what? The past? Conflicting emotions?

Standing in front of the stove, Gwendolyn

tapped a slotted spoon on the side of a pan to get his attention. "How hungry are you?"

"Not at all," he admitted. The only thing that sounded very appealing was a strong drink. "Pamela Jo told me something unexpected tonight."

"Oh?"

"She's an alcoholic."

His mother pointed the spoon at him. "Possible ammo against her in case she ever tries to take Faith."

He scowled, a little irritated that his mom's immediate reaction was how to use the information to her advantage. *Technically,* my *advantage.* She was only trying to protect him and Faith. Still… "I don't think that's going to be a problem. She's not after custody." Hell, he'd practically had to beg to get her to agree to half an hour with their daughter, which reminded him all too painfully of when Faith had been a baby. When he hadn't been busy trying to appease his parents, he'd been trying to cajole his wife into taking an interest in her own child. *"I'll change her diaper, but wouldn't you like to hold her afterward?"*

"Besides," he told his mom, "she's a *recovering* alcoholic. She mentioned looking for AA meetings while she's in town. That sounds like pretty responsible behavior to me." It wasn't as if she'd been doing lines of coke on her aunt's front porch. "I was just surprised to hear that she'd had problems drinking because of her mother. She was always so embarrassed and angry about Mae, I figured Pamela Jo would be the last person in the world to hit the bottle."

Gwendolyn shrugged. "You hear statistics about children of abusive or alcoholic parents being more likely to become abusive or alcoholics themselves. I'm more surprised that she confided something so personal." The critical edge in her voice was unmistakable.

"You have an overactive imagination," he scoffed, aware that *imaginative* was not how most people would characterize Gwendolyn Shepard. "We spoke briefly on her aunt and uncle's front porch. It was by no means an intimate chat."

"Good," his mother said unapologetically. "Because the last thing you need is to get involved with that woman again!"

"Mimosa is more likely to be wiped off the planet by an asteroid," he assured her wryly. "We're...strangers now. Who don't much like each other." He'd been exasperated by Pamela Jo's reminders to call her Pam, as if she could erase the past and make herself a different person just by shortening her name.

But she *was* a different person, wasn't she? One who'd apparently developed and fought an addiction he'd known nothing about. What about the other details of her life? Had she, like Nick, remarried? Where did she even call home these days?

He only knew one thing about her absolutely. Pam had given him Faith, for which he would always be grateful. And he wouldn't breathe easy again until Pam left Mimosa.

Chapter Seven

By the time AA ended, the sun had fully set. The bobwhites that had been singing when Pam had parked her car an hour ago had been replaced with the harmonious buzz of insects and the low hoot of a distant owl. Even though it was dark, she'd decided to visit Mae's grave. The idea had come to her during the meeting, when she'd been thinking what a waste it was that alcoholism was probably the strongest bond she and Mae had ever shared. She knew that if she waited until morning, Ed or Julia would probably insist on coming with her, wanting to be there for her, but she preferred to do this alone.

Pam had seen big, formal cemeteries before

that were gated and locked up after a certain hour. But Mae had been buried in the small patch of graveyard alongside the old Baptist church, which had been a one-room schoolhouse many decades before and had gradually lost a fair amount of its congregation to newer churches in the area. Anyone could park at the church and walk between the headstones.

The uneven parking lot was empty at this hour, and Pam pulled up as close as she could to the edge of the cemetery. She climbed out of the car, leaving her headlights on for illumination. The headstones closest were the ones that had been there longest, so she automatically went to the back row, looking for a stone not so weathered by time. Even though she had to squint to read it, she made out her mother's name. Mae Danvers Wilson, Mother and Sister.

Pam swallowed, turning the words over in her head—especially the "mother" part. "You weren't much good at it," she said candidly. The sentiment might be disrespectful of the dead, but it was still true. "Wherever you are now, I hope you know I came back. I wanted to see you."

The odds weren't good that they would have hugged it out and gone on to be lifelong friends, but whatever happened would have been better than *this,* this piercing sense of incompleteness.

This hollow feeling of unfinished business was a major reason she'd agreed to Nick's request this afternoon. Pam wasn't worthy of being anyone's mom—she hadn't even been sober a full year—but if letting Faith meet her would give the girl any kind of closure, then her daughter deserved it.

"Your granddaughter's beautiful," Pam said. Seeing that school picture had been a jolt, like banging a funny bone against a doorjamb. Tingly and painful all at once. Pam almost envied Mae for the years she'd spent in Mimosa, theoretically able to watch Faith from afar. Truthfully, though, Pam doubted her mother had crawled out of the bottle long enough to care that she was a grandmother. And Pam knew without a doubt that the Shepards never would have let Mae, who'd disowned Pam and hadn't even attended the wedding, anywhere near Faith. *Rightfully so.* Faith should be protected from selfish, destructive alcoholics.

Pam took a deep breath. "I'm trying to forgive you, Mom. Some days I'm better at it than others. I wish things could have been different." She stopped, then felt foolish, as if she were waiting for a response she knew would never come. "I don't know how long I'll be in Mimosa, but I'll come back again. I'll bring flowers next time."

Blinking against the glare of the headlights,

Pam made her way back to the car. Flowers would help alleviate the grimness of the stark, simple stone. *Mae Danvers Wilson, Mother and Sister.* If Pam had somehow killed herself during the worst of her drinking, she wouldn't even have had that much to claim. She'd never had a sister and she'd completely forfeited her right to be a mother. Still, she thanked God that she'd realized something was unnaturally wrong with her in time, that she hadn't stuck around to damage her own daughter. She wanted Faith to grow up secure in Nick's love and the adoration of all the Shepards; she never wanted *her* daughter to be the one standing in a dark cemetery with decades worth of bad memories and self-doubt.

"Structurally sound, but needs a lot of work. And a lot of love."

Pam slanted Ed a sidelong glance. *Is he talking about the house or me?* As a guest in her aunt and uncle's home for the last couple of days, she'd realized there was a lot more to the man than she'd guessed. As a teen, she'd viewed him as the henpecked, somewhat simpleminded husband of an overbearing woman. But this week she'd witnessed the subtle affection between the couple. Also, she'd learned that while

Uncle Ed didn't talk much, his words often carried more than their superficial meaning.

The man was eerily insightful. She suspected that when she'd said she was going out for a drive to see how the town had changed, he'd somehow known she was going to an AA meeting at a nearby church. Pam had been slow to broach the subject with them because Julia was still so obviously upset by her late sister's drinking and alcohol-related death.

Ed turned off the car. "Your inheritance awaits."

They'd met with the attorney this morning, and Pam was the proud owner of one forlorn, neglected house. *Last week, all I had to my name was the car, and now I'm a regular land baron.* Oh, yeah, things were looking up.

Uncle Ed had discreetly handed her a check for "miscellaneous" costs, like taxes, realty fees and maintenance. But from where she stood, this place needed more than "miscellaneous" repair.

"That additional money you gave me wasn't from Mae," she said as they exited the car. "You tried to make it sound that way, as if you were just holding it in trust for me as executors of the 'estate.' But there's no way she had that much."

"The money's for you, from family who want

to help. Who would have been helping all along if we'd had the opportunity. Don't worry, our savings are in good shape." He shook his head. "I had no idea how well your aunt was going to do with her jewelry-making and craft shows."

"I appreciate the help," Pam said softly. It would have been less humbling to turn the check down, but she'd learned the value of accepting assistance.

"It's up to you, of course, how you spend it. You could try to buy a listing for the property and sell the place as-is…or you could invest some time and cash and ask a much better price. Isn't that what they call 'flipping' a house?"

"Mmm." She didn't know much about house-flipping, but she was pretty sure no one who was good at it would have picked this particular home. It didn't offer some of the amenities that were considered standard on newer houses—like a garage—and it wasn't part of a neighborhood where it could be buoyed by adjacent property values. But she was basing her low expectations on a cursory inspection of the house's exterior. The inside might be more promising.

Then again. A few minutes later, Pam stood in the kitchen, reevaluating. The inside sucked.

"It could be worse," Uncle Ed said from behind her.

"Oh, there's a ringing endorsement. I think that's how the property listing should read." Although now that she thought about it, the house might not even qualify for a listing. Didn't houses have to pass certain minimal inspections before they could legally be sold? She didn't think the walls were full of asbestos, but it was apparent from the damaged patches in the ceiling that the roof needed work. There were definite plumbing issues, too, from the minor problem that faucets caked with mineral deposits would need to be replaced to the less minor news from Uncle Ed that tree roots had grown through some of the underground pipes. Carpeting and windows needed to be replaced. Vents and ducts needed to be professionally cleaned.

Appearance-wise, the kitchen was the most depressing. The damaged tiles and hollowed-out section of counter told a story of a dishwasher that had leaked water all over the floor and had eventually been removed, but never replaced. Ugly colored paint was peeling off the cabinets, and one or two of the cabinet doors had become so warped they no longer closed properly.

Pam's lungs constricted in a moment of panicked defeatism. *Mae's parting gift... I always knew she hated me.*

"It's doable," Ed said, his quiet voice firm.

There was something hushed about the rooms around them that encouraged whispering, like a library. Or a haunted house. "It will be hard, sure, but you've survived much harder, haven't you?"

She studied him, temporarily distracted from the two-bedroom, one-and-a-half-bath albatross around her neck, wondering how much he'd intuited about her. "How do you know my life hasn't been all rainbows and rose petals?" she joked weakly.

"We took my car today because you weren't sure yours would start. And your aunt Julia, who has only been outside the state of Mississippi a half-dozen times, owns an entire matched set of floral upholstered suitcases, while your luggage seems to consist of backpacks and recycled grocery bags. You look like you haven't eaten in a year, and your eyes…" He trailed off, and she didn't press him for more grim detail. She wasn't sure she wanted to hear it.

"Busted. It hasn't been all rose petals," she confirmed. "Although, for a while, I did try to find rainbows at the bottom of beer steins and shot glasses. I'm an alcoholic."

He nodded. "Runs in your family. Your great-grandfather and great-uncle both were."

"I didn't know that." She'd grown up painfully aware that her mother had a problem—the entire town had known Mae had a problem—but she'd never questioned whether previous relatives had shared the same vices.

"You got it under control?" he asked.

"For now." To assume that she had it under control permanently, or to pretend there weren't days she struggled, would be worse than arrogance; it would be stupidity.

"You planning to tell your aunt?"

With Aunt Julia being a devout teetotaler—literally—the subject might never occur naturally in her house. "Eventually, I guess. It's not that I'm trying to lie to her, it's just difficult."

Ed patted her shoulder. "Let me know what I can do to help. Now, about the hinges on these cabinets…"

Having dispensed with personal conversation, they spent the next forty minutes cataloguing and discussing the house's many flaws and few attributes—the wiring was in good shape, and both the bedrooms had ceiling fans.

"If you didn't want to sell the house outright," Ed began as she locked the front door, "you could always rent it to someone. That would keep it in the family. And if you wanted to partially furnish it, I know someone who could get you some great discounts." He winked.

She smiled fondly at him, knowing that his owning a furniture warehouse was how Julia had managed to afford many of her favorite pieces. "Thank you. It's a generous offer, but I don't think I'm landlord material." If she rented out the house, it would become an ongoing responsibility, a tether to a place she didn't want to be. "No, I'm going to fix it up, then sell."

"Either way, we get to enjoy your company for a while." Ed glanced from her to the house. "Repairs of this magnitude could take weeks. Months, depending on how much you tackle yourself and how much we delegate. Why don't you spend the next day or so putting together a list of what you want to accomplish? Then I can recommend places or people to use. I'd offer to roll up my sleeves and help you get started this weekend, but I promised to drive your aunt up to Rowlett for a jewelry expo on Saturday. You're welcome to come with us."

"Thanks, but I have a previous engagement. Dawn offered to do my hair at the salon." Which was entirely true. But there was also the far scarier appointment to meet Faith on Saturday. Nick had insisted they wait until the weekend, instead of throwing something potentially upsetting at his daughter in the midst of her school week. Far from resenting the delay, Pam applauded his paternal vigilance. Maybe, given the extra time, he'd come to his senses and cancel the meeting altogether.

But she rather doubted it.

"How do I look, Dad?"

Nick raised his eyes from his laptop and the monthly bills he'd been paying to find his daughter in the doorway. She'd braided her hair and was wearing a baggy T-shirt printed with the logo of one of her favorite bands over a pair of black jeans. Before he had a chance to say anything, Faith sighed.

"Too teenager, right? Jeans and a T-shirt, ultimate cliché. I have a pair of capris clean, but they were *eulcgh*." She demonstrated her distaste for said capris with a derisive, phlegmy sound. She blushed, adding quickly, "Not that I'm worried about impressing her! I don't care what her opinion is. You think a skirt? Yeah, probably a skirt."

Despite any momentary bravado about "not caring," Nick knew Faith was far too emotionally invested in a single milk shake date. He hoped she had realistic expectations about the outcome. He forced himself to keep a light tone rather than reissue any of the cautionary reminders he'd been giving since she'd learned her mother was in town. "Fashion advice from the old man, huh? So I'm like your Michael Garcia now."

Judging from her vacant stare, his analogy hadn't been as fitting as he'd hoped. "Isn't he one of the judges from that runway show you watched over the summer?" He'd come home from work a couple of times to find her and Morgan engrossed in a marathon of repeats.

She threw him a pitying look. "Close, but no. Do I have time to go change?"

He was torn between telling her to take all the time she needed and urging her to hurry; the longer they left Pam sitting there all alone, the greater the chance she might talk herself into bolting.

"Go put on whatever you'll be most comfortable in," he advised his daughter, "but do it fast. I know how you hate being late."

A few minutes later, Faith spun back into the room in a brightly patterned top and denim skirt. Somewhere along the way, she'd also pulled the braid loose; her long hair was still kinked into ripples where it had been plaited together. "Ready," she sang.

That makes one of us. "All right." He stood. "Just let me grab my keys, and—"

"Got 'em!" She jangled the key ring in her

hand. "And your wallet's on the counter. You can get it on our way out the door. Let's go!"

Tension pinched the back of Nick's neck. One would think they were on their way to a circus, or—realizing that she was a young woman now and not a happy-go-lucky six-year-old—some kind of sweepstakes giveaway shopping spree. Faith gave no sign of being on her way to meet a mother who had ditched her and then never bothered to send so much as a birthday card for the next twelve years. He prayed his daughter would be the same person on the other side of this meeting, that however Pam answered the girl's questions, she would do so with gentle diplomacy. It would kill him for Faith to feel unwanted or unworthy.

Mimosa was not a big town—you could generally get from any Point A to Point B in under fifteen minutes. But today, it seemed like they made their trip in three. Not a single light turned red in their path, no cars pulled in front of them on the narrow roads.

The moment of reckoning had come.

Faith yanked off her seat belt while he was still parking. "Do you think she's already here? Do you think I'll be taller than her? These boots have a heel on them. You're not staying, right?"

"We've already been over that," he grumbled. Could his daughter make it any clearer that she wanted him nowhere on the premises? He'd agreed to go across the street and browse the hardware store to give the two ladies their privacy. "But I'll have my cell phone in my hand the whole time. Yours is charged, right?"

She rolled her eyes. "Of course, Dad."

"Call me or text me if you—"

"Relax," she teased. "I'm the one who should be nervous. You already know this woman."

He held open the door to the diner for Faith, scanning the room over the top of her head to see if he spotted—*Thank you, God.* The bunched muscles in his neck and shoulders unclenched when he saw Pam sitting in a booth over to the side. Even though she'd given her word, he'd had his doubts that she would follow through.

"There," he told his daughter softly. "That's her."

Faith stopped so suddenly in the entrance that he almost tripped over her. He gave her shoulder a squeeze of encouragement, and she was off again. Even though his legs were far longer, he had to quicken his stride to keep up with her.

Pam had stood, rising to meet them. She lifted a hand to just below her shoulder, where it fluttered for a moment before dropping to her side.

He recognized the incomplete gesture; she used to fiddle with the ends of her hair all the time. Faith did, too—when she was little, if she'd been feeling shy, she actually stretched her hair in front of her face. Maybe it was a girl thing.

Pam smiled tremulously at their daughter. "You must be Faith."

She nodded. "Hi, M—" Abruptly she swung her gaze back to Nick, asking in a stage whisper, "What do I call her?"

"Pam," he said. "Pam Wilson, meet Faith Shepard."

Pam cleared her throat. "Won't you have a seat?"

With one last nervous glance at her dad, Faith slid into the booth opposite her birth mother. Nick took that as his cue to make himself scarce.

"If you two don't need me, I have some errands over at the hardware store. Just across the street," he reminded his daughter. He didn't want her to forget for a second that he was close if she needed him.

Faith nodded impatiently, but Pam looked stricken. "You're not staying?" she asked.

"I thought the two of you would rather chat alone. Girl talk."

After a second's hesitation, Pam nodded gamely. "Of course."

Despite her even tone, her expression was unmistakable. He would know it anywhere because he'd seen that same expression countless times in his own reflection: *Don't let me screw this up.* Parenting—particularly parenting a soon-to-be teenage girl—was like juggling flaming objects while walking a tightrope blindfolded with no safety net. Even if it was only for thirty minutes, Pam was getting a taste of what he experienced every day. Feeling an unexpected bond with her at that moment, he smiled at her. She smiled back, and he had the oddest realization.

He'd relegated Pam Wilson and her role in his life to former love. It had never occurred to him that she might still be someone he could like.

Finally. Faith had felt like her dad would never leave! Now that he was gone, she turned eagerly to study her mother across the table.

When Faith had been little, her father gave her a picture frame, the kind that held multiple photos and had a little kickstand on back so it would stand up on a shelf or piece of furniture. That frame held the only three pictures she had of her mom. One was a shot of her mom sitting on a picnic blanket by some water; another was of her dad and Pam's wedding day. It hadn't looked like a fancy ceremony—he was only in a jacket and tie, not a tuxedo, and the gown had been a simple yellow dress with lacy sleeves and beading on the bodice. They were so young, it looked more like someone's prom picture than a wedding photo. But they'd been smiling happily at each other. Faith's remaining picture was from right after she was born. Her parents were sitting on Grandma Gwendolyn's couch, and her dad was holding her. She hated that one. No one looked happy in it, especially Faith, whose face was screwed up into a red scowl. She was obviously about to cry.

She'd asked Grandma Gwendolyn once if she'd cried a lot as a baby, but her grandmother assured her she'd been an "angel." Faith wasn't stupid. If she'd been such an angel, why had her mother left her? She could ask Pam that very question, but her stomach knotted. Faith wasn't sure she was brave enough to hear the answer.

"You look different than I thought," Faith said. "Different than in the pictures, I mean."

Pam smiled, but it looked kind of fake. "Imagine how I feel. You look a lot different than in my picture, too."

My picture? Surely Pam didn't mean she only had one. "You're pretty," Faith said timidly. It probably sounded like she was just sucking up, but it was true. Even though Faith liked long hair, she thought her mom looked good with shorter hair. And although Pam wasn't wearing makeup and was way older than she'd been on her wedding day, she was still a lot prettier than Morgan's mom—a single woman who always flirted with Faith's dad whenever he came to pick her up from her friend's house.

Pam laughed, and her smile seemed more natural now. "Thanks. Back atcha, kid. So—" she toyed with the laminated menu "—you hungry? We could order food or split an appetizer if you want. Or just stick to the shakes. There's nothing bad on this menu."

"What's your favorite flavor of milk shake?" Faith asked, hoping her mother would say cookies and cream. That was Faith's favorite.

"Plain old chocolate. In my opinion, it's hard to improve on a classic."

"Oh." Well, that was okay. Faith and Morgan didn't like all the same stuff, either. "Just a milk shake for me, please. I already ate lunch."

Pam nodded, then waved to the waitress. They started to place their order, but Faith interrupted, pulling out her phone.

"Hold on!" She hit the camera function on the menu screen. "I want the waitress to take a picture of us. You don't mind, do you?"

Pam seemed surprised by the request, but not angry. "No, that's fine."

Faith breathed a sigh of relief. "Great." Both of them leaned across the table, so that their heads were close together in the center, and smiled at the waitress. "Thank you." *Now I have four.*

Pam was in awe of the way her adolescent companion managed to down a shake yet never stop talking. Pam's own milk shake had melted into a sad chocolaty puddle while she tried to keep up with Faith's questions. Most of them were blessedly superficial—what was Pam's favorite color, had any of Faith's teachers taught at the middle school back when Pam was a student there?—but a few had been more heavy-hitting.

"Why did you…" Faith hesitated, bending her straw back and forth with such intense focus that Pam expected it to snap. "What made you agree to meet me?"

"It's the least I owe you," Pam said quietly. "To tell the truth, I'm surprised you wanted to. I wouldn't blame you if you hated me."

Faith frowned, then said with a directness that sounded much like her father's, "Only sometimes."

The two of them locked gazes, neither sure what to say. If Pam tried to explain the paralyzing depression that had engulfed her after she'd given birth to Faith, would the girl somehow feel responsible? Pam would rather say nothing and let her daughter be angry than risk Faith blaming herself.

"At least," Faith blurted suddenly, as if unnerved by the silence, "divorce is a clean, honest break. Not like what Jenna did when she cheated on Dad. She was his wife in North Carolina."

"Do you miss her?" Pam asked. After all, that woman had been far more of a mother than she herself had.

"I don't know. Most of the time I'm cool with it being just Dad and me."

The words warmed Pam. *I knew he'd be a good father.* Even in the short while she'd shared Faith with him, she'd glimpsed it. One Nick as a parent was worth twenty of Pam in the same situation.

"But then something will happen," Faith continued, "that he gets weird about. You know, girl stuff, so he makes me talk to Grandma Gwendolyn or Aunt Leigh. I love them, but Aunt Leigh only has sons, and Grandma Gwendolyn…"

Been there. No one had to explain to Pam

how difficult Gwendolyn Shepard could be. Pam should steer the conversation in a different direction before she ended up saying something she regretted about the girl's grandmother. "Your dad tells me you have a great singing voice. Do you plan to pursue that?"

"Pursue? Like how?"

"Voice lessons or high school choral group or maybe singing professionally one day."

"I don't know. It would be such a cool job to star in one of those musicals that tours all over the place, so I could travel to lots of cities. But I think what I want to do is get a job at NASA in Alabama. Dad took me to the Marshall Space Flight Center, and it rocked."

Pam leaned back in her booth. If she'd been harboring any delusions that Faith was a Mini Me, they'd just been blown out of the water. Pam had barely passed her math and science courses in high school; even if she had, she never would have thought a career using those skills was exciting. *This kid sounds more together at twelve than I was throughout my twenties.* "I'm impressed. You must be really good in school."

"I am!" Inexplicably the girl sounded exasperated. "Which is what I keep telling Dad. I'm an A student, so he and Grandma Gwendolyn should ease up. They don't need to be on my case all the time like I'm some kind of delinquent."

Pam bit her lip. Gwendolyn's son had knocked up his teenage girlfriend. Had Nick and Pam's past behavior caused her to err on the side of prison warden when it came to her granddaughter? And while Pam knew in her bones that Nick adored Faith and would do anything for her, it wasn't difficult to imagine him being overprotective. Didn't he understand that kids who felt suffocated by rules and regulations were often the ones who rebelled? Pam couldn't stand to think of the bright, beautiful girl across the table doing something stupid that would mar her future just because she felt the need to defy her elders.

A chiming sound came from Faith's phone. She glanced at the screen and sighed. "Dad just texted. He's on his way. Must be thirty minutes on the dot. He's kind of a stickler."

Half an hour had passed already. Pam wasn't sure how she felt about that. On the one hand, their conversation hadn't been nearly as excruciating as she'd anticipated. On the other, she'd had the underlying sensation of walking on eggshells this entire time, afraid that the next thing she said might be the wrong one, and she was looking forward to being able to breathe normally again.

"Thank you for the milk shake," Faith said, her formal manner making her suddenly seem more childlike. A little girl hosting a tea party for imagined royalty. "And for answering my questions. I only have one more. Don't you think everyone should have a mother?" She kept her tone carefully neutral, as if she were asking in the abstract rather than about herself.

Ignoring the pang in her midsection—under wildly different circumstances, could she have been a real mother to this girl?—Pam chose her words carefully. "In a perfect world, sure. But in reality, maybe it's better sometimes not to have a mom than to have one who's terrible." Images of Mae flashed through Pam's mind. It was occasionally difficult to remember what the woman had looked like smiling, but it was second nature to envision her raging drunkenly about how Pam had ruined her life.

Faith straightened, her face alert and anxious. "Were you a terrible mom?"

I was going to be. "Oh, there's your dad."

Faith craned her neck, looking back toward the door. She heaved a sigh, clearly not sharing Pam's ambivalence that their visit was over. "Goodbye."

Rather surprised by the lump in her throat and how hard it was to get out a farewell, Pam nodded in response. By the time Nick reached the table, she was able to add, "Take care of yourself. And listen to your father."

Faith crossed her eyes and made a face.

"Hey!" Nick reached out to playfully tap his daughter on the shoulder. "What happened to respecting your seniors?"

"Sorry." Faith giggled, clearly not.

"You ready to go?" he prompted.

Obediently she stood, but then threw one last imploring glance at Pam. "Maybe I can see you again?"

Behind Faith, Nick's eyes turned to thunderclouds. He'd been all right with this as an isolated event but obviously didn't want it to turn into a habit.

"Not unless we happen to run into each other," Pam said, trying to take the sting out of her refusal. "I won't be in Mimosa long, and I'm going to be really busy while I'm here. But I'll never forget today." That was the gospel truth.

For almost two straight years, Pam's existence had blurred together in hazy, kaleidoscope episodes, broken up by periodic hangovers and rare moments of clarity and self-loathing when she faced a counter full of empty bottles and had to admit that they could all be attributed to her. There was a lot she didn't remember. And a lot she did she wished she couldn't.

What Faith had given her today, this single half hour that Pam would carry with her for the rest of her life—that alone had been worth getting sober.

Chapter Eight

Nick had a case of the Saturday night blues, a restless dissatisfaction, marked by a lot of pacing and grouchiness and the world's shortest attention span. In his early twenties, he'd struggled with this every week, the sense that everyone he knew was out somewhere having a good time, while he was trapped at home. He'd outgrown that long before meeting Jenna. Now that he was single again, if someone were to ask, he'd say that after a long week, he was perfectly happy to rent a movie and split a pizza with his kid, then call it a night.

Not that the "kid" was so happy with that arrangement, he thought wryly. Faith had kept to herself for most of the afternoon, and he hadn't wanted to press her for details about her conversation with Pam. His daughter knew he was here and would talk to him when she was ready. When she'd bounced down the stairs before dinner, he'd misinterpreted her sudden presence as exactly that.

But it hadn't been him she'd wanted to confide in—she'd asked for permission to spend the night at Morgan's.

He'd felt like an ogre as he reminded her, "You're grounded." In his humble opinion, Morgan should be, too.

"These are extenuating circumstances!" Faith had argued, breaking out the PSAT vocabulary words. She sometimes did that when she was trying to get her way, as if more highbrow language would convince him to take her seriously. "I had the first encounter I can remember with my mother today, probably the only one I'll *ever* have. I need to talk to a friend."

"You could talk to me," he'd suggested.

This was met with a roll of the eyes and a huffy sigh as she stomped out of the room.

When the phone rang two hours later, he found himself almost wishing he'd capitulated. If Faith were out of the house Nick could take Joseph Anders up on his offer.

"Thanks for the invite," Nick told his co-worker, "but I can't. It's a little late in the evening for me to call up Mom or Leigh and ask them to come over last minute." The problem with grounding your kid was that you effectively grounded yourself, too.

"Any other weekend, you could drop Faith off at my house. Lisa would probably welcome the company," Joseph said of his wife. "But she and the twins are visiting her parents in Kentucky. Damn shame you can't join us. I like Tully, but the man can't bowl worth squat. Without you, we're the odds-on favorite to lose."

"Sorry, guy. Check with me next time, though." Nick hung up the phone, admitting to himself that, even if he'd gone, he wouldn't have been much help to Joseph's cause. He was far too preoccupied tonight.

There had been rumblings in the hardware store where he'd gone to give Faith and Pam their space. Apparently, Ed Calbert had come in yesterday with his prodigal niece and placed a sizable order. Although Nick had heard months ago that Mae Wilson died, he hadn't thought much about her leaving Pam anything. Frankly he was a bit surprised to learn she'd had any-thing *to* leave. But now he realized that Pam owned the old house and would need to do con-

siderable repairs if she was to have any hope
of selling it.

Which meant that Pam wasn't going anywhere just yet.

Hell, I run a construction company. If he
volunteered to work for half-price, would she
be gone sooner? Or he could just bulldoze the
place for her. Judging from the occasional
glimpses he caught from the road, it wouldn't
take much to flatten the neglected place into
nothingness. Some things couldn't be saved; it
might be better just to start over, rebuild.

He could just imagine the look on Gwendolyn's face if he told his mother he was helping
Pam renovate a house. The back of her head
would blow off. He almost grinned at the rare
prospect of his mother speechless.

Nick had muted a ballgame on television
when Joseph called. Now he restored sound
with the remote but still couldn't concentrate.
He ended up in the kitchen, randomly opening
cabinets and inspecting refrigerator shelves with
cursory interest. *Boredom munchies.* He didn't
really want to eat. He wanted something physical to do, something that would help him work
off this prowling sense of…whatever it was.

He opened the high cabinet above the refrigerator and reached for the bottle of premium whiskey his semiretired boss, Donald Bauer, had given him at Christmas. As Nick headed for the dishwasher to get a clean tumbler, he noticed Faith's phone on the counter. He pulled the spare charger out of a drawer. He reminded her on a near daily basis that the phone whose chief purpose was supposed to have been "for emergencies" wasn't going to do her any good if it ran out of juice and couldn't be used in an actual crisis. There was a bloop of acknowledgment when he plugged in the phone, and the dark screen brightened. Instead of the usual wallpaper, a picture of Faith and Morgan making crazy faces on the back porch, there was a photo of Faith and Pam, heads close together over a dark green tabletop, smiling at the camera.

He sucked in a breath at the unexpected vision.

They really did look a lot alike. In an alternate reality, this would have been a picture *he'd* taken—a routine family outing, a spontaneous shot of his wife and daughter. His throat tightened, and he ran his thumb across the picture, enlarging it so that it was zoomed in on Pam. Her face and hair and style were different, but her eyes hadn't changed at all.

When they'd been together, he'd found it boldly erotic that she so frequently met his gaze during sex. Her lashes didn't close often, and she rarely turned her head away from him. Instead she looked right into him.

With a groan, he set down the phone and guiltily shoved it away. Then he poured himself a double. Watching the alcohol splash into the glass kept his thoughts centered on her. Did Pam ever get this itchy, restless feeling? He was vaguely aware that Ed and Julia were gone most weekends; was Pam all alone in that house?

He pulled his own cell phone out of his pocket and padded barefoot onto the back porch. She'd called him the other day to confirm the time she was meeting Faith. Scrolling through recent calls, he clicked on the only one that was unfamiliar before he could stop to question his actions.

The phone rang twice and, without thinking, he greeted her the way he always had—ever since he'd asked her to be his homecoming date sophomore year. "Hey, it's me." As if taking for granted that she'd recognize him instantly, as if no time had passed.

"Hey." Her voice was breathy, low, reminding him of all the times they'd been on the phone after midnight and she hadn't wanted her mother to catch her.

They'd had some intense late-night discussions about whether or not they were "ready to go all the way." They'd anticipated what it would be like, and some of those graphic conversations had been a lot hotter than their actual first time, which had ended too soon. Of course, they'd improved greatly with practice.

"Nick, you still there?"

He tossed back a swallow of whiskey. "I'm here."

"Good. I'm glad you called."

He'd been expecting more wariness—or even exasperation—and her welcoming tone knocked him off balance.

"Saves me the trouble of finding your card again," she continued. "I wanted to talk."

"You did?" Nick set his drink down on the picnic table he'd built. Pam's voice in his ear had more kick to it than the whiskey; both at the same time were too potent. He needed to keep a clear head.

"Well, to say thank you, first of all. For today."

"So you don't think I'm a bully anymore for trying to talk you into it?"

She was quiet for a long moment, as if giving his words serious consideration. "I have a friend I think you would like. Annabel. She's a firm believer in an unapologetic kick in the ass, if it's warranted."

"Happy to help." He paced the grass along the edge of the porch, the ground cool and damp against his bare feet. "You said 'first of all.' Was there more than one reason you were planning to call me?" Was it possible his mother's insane suspicions weren't so insane—could Pam have missed him? After all, they were both back in Mimosa, where certain nostalgic tendencies might take effect.

But Pam sounded far from wistfully reminiscent when she said, "It's about Faith."

His body tensed. "What about her?"

"I realize this is none of my business..." Utterly bizarre words for a girl's mother to be speaking, but given the circumstances, accurate. "She seems like a good kid."

"The best."

"So you might want to consider, um, easing up on her. A bit." Her discomfort seeped through the phone lines. Doling out unsolicited advice did not come as easily to her as it did to Gwendolyn and Leigh.

"Easing up? Did she paint me as some sort of über-strict parent?" *The little con artist.* It galled him to think that after he'd faced down

Pam, not to mention his mother, to get Faith today's opportunity, she'd used it to bitch about him.

"Actually, she seemed to adore you. She said she was even cool most of the time with not having a mom because she had you. I got the impression it had more to do with Gwendolyn."

Ah. That he could believe.

"And that she just wants you to trust her, to give her the space to prove she'll make smart decisions."

He snorted. "And did this upstanding citizen mention to you that she's currently grounded for cutting class?"

"She what?"

It was gratifying to hear his own parental outrage echoed. "Oh, so she left out that part when she was describing life under my tyrannical thumb."

Pam sighed. "Damn it—*darn* it, I knew I should have stayed out of it. I've just... I was in California for a while and ran into lots of people making bad decisions. Some of them started as good kids with promising futures, but they rebelled too far against the restrictive ways they were being raised. Parents who probably thought they were keeping their children from harm inadvertently pushed them into it. I'm sure the last thing you want is for Faith to end up, well, like I did."

The idea of his daughter as a pregnant teenager was enough to wake him in the middle of the night drenched in a cold sweat. He pushed it aside and focused on Pam instead. "Are you saying that's what I was to you, teenage rebellion? A method for getting back at your mom?"

"No!" She quickly shot down his idle theory. "Are you kidding? We were together for years, Nick. I've had one-night stands, mistakes that made me ashamed to look at myself in the mirror the next day. That's not what... I loved you."

His jaw clenched. How dare she say that to him, this woman who'd whispered words of love to him for years, then disappeared? He'd seen her once, on television, and had been incensed that she'd simply built a new life without a backward glance at him and Faith. Why hadn't it been that easy for him, to forget the woman who'd betrayed him? Instead, Pam had waltzed through his mind so many times she'd worn her own groove.

Not that he planned to share that with her. "I shouldn't have called."

"Why did you?" Now the wariness he'd anticipated had crept into her tone.

"Who the hell knows?" He leaned back, taking in the inky black night. The way he was feeling, there should have been a full moon. "I get antsy sometimes, on edge, and I thought you might feel that way on late Saturday nights, too. I heard your aunt and uncle were out of town, and you met Faith today…"

"So you were calling to check on me?" She sounded bemused. "To make sure I wasn't raiding the liquor cabinet? Not that Aunt Julia has one."

"Something like that. I didn't really analyze it, just dialed." How many times would he have called her over the years if he'd had a number? "Don't worry, it won't happen again."

The stress headache behind Pam's left eye throbbed in time to the bass-heavy pop song playing through the salon's speakers. On Sundays, the place was only open for a few hours in the afternoon. It was due to close in about fifteen minutes. Given the day Pam was having so far, she'd debated telling Dawn she was unfit company and canceling. But at the last minute, Pam had reconsidered. Visiting her old friend gave her a much-needed excuse to head into town. Because if she'd stayed at the house any longer, she couldn't be held responsible for her actions.

When she'd staggered bleary-eyed from her bed this morning, she'd actually been looking forward to tackling Mae's house. It might be a lengthy, complicated process, but at least there weren't emotions and verbal land mines involved. Instead of letting herself be overwhelmed by the house as a whole, she'd tried to break down a list of individual projects.

Unfortunately very few of them could be completed in a day, and when she added up the cost of all of those projects...

Even with no major living expenses while she stayed with her relatives and Uncle Ed's generous seed money for renovation, the expense was daunting. She'd decided around lunchtime that if she could just accomplish *one* tangible thing, she'd feel inspired. She'd chosen the handle on the back door, which needed to be replaced because, as she'd discovered when she'd been rinsing off some stuff in the yard, the door wouldn't open at all from the outside. It had seemed simple enough—until she shattered the glass in the sliding door.

Now she had two small butterfly bandages across the tender flesh between her thumb and index finger and a large sheet of plastic across the gaping hole that used to be a door. Plus her list of projects had just increased by one.

She'd had disturbing visions of herself on the front page of the *Mimosa Monitor,* pictured wild-eyed above an article about arson.

All I wanted to do was fix the dang door handle! Is that really so much to ask? Apparently, yes. All she had to do was be patient. If today's success was any indication, the house would be a pile of rubble by the end of the week.

"There you are!" Dawn's friendly greeting was just below shriek decibel, and Pam struggled to smile instead of wince. "Glad to see you took me up on my offer. Just give me a few minutes. We're shorthanded today and it's been crazy. I need to put some stuff in the computer and sweep up." She jerked a thumb toward the styling stations behind her.

The floor at one booth was dusted with brown hair, so short that Pam guessed the chair had been occupied by a male client getting a trim. In the next seat over was a redhead with a handful of tissues; she was sniffling about her louse of an ex-boyfriend and periodically instructing the smocked hairdresser to "lop it all off!" Judging by the pile of strawberry locks accumulating in the floor, the hairdresser was doing exactly that.

Put a blonde in the third chair, and the checker-board tile would have a new neopolitan theme.

Pressing a hand to the small of her back, Pam volunteered, "I could sweep if you want." It would be visible progress—an easily defined and accomplished job. In other words, the opposite of everything else she'd done today.

"You sure you don't mind?" Dawn asked.

Lowering her voice discreetly, Pam said, "I'm getting a free haircut out of the deal. Sweeping is the least I can do!"

"Okay, then." Dawn smiled brightly and retrieved a broom from the spacious storage closet on the other side of the reception counter. "Appreciate the help. One of our girls is pregnant, and she had to go to the E.R. last night. She should be all right, but the doctor has her on bed rest for the remainder of her last trimester! Which means we're going to be shorthanded for September homecoming, when pretty much every female student at Mimosa High School comes in for an updo and all the women over thirty come to get their gray covered before the alumni luncheon. I don't suppose you're a licensed cosmetologist?"

Pam laughed. "Hardly. But I wield a mean broom." She got to work sweeping, surprised to discover that her headache receded from excruciatingly unbearable to just annoyingly painful.

Her skull had throbbed for pretty much the past twenty-four hours. Although she'd enjoyed talking to Faith far more than she'd expected, it had been difficult to spend that time with her daughter. Last night Pam had been plagued with uncharacteristic what-ifs. She'd been unable to reach Annabel and had tortured herself with not only the milestones she'd already missed in Faith's life—first step, first loose tooth, first day of school—but also the ones still to come. Her high school graduation, her wedding day.

It hadn't helped Pam's conflicted emotional state that Nick had called. Checking on her seemed chivalrous, despite his surliness by the end of their conversation, and she didn't deserve gallantry from Nick. It only served to confuse her. Considering his eventual return to hostility, maybe he was confused, too.

"Uh, did we hire someone new and no one told me?"

Pam turned to see a skinny woman in head-to-toe black emerge from a room at the far end of the salon.

The background staccato of keyboard typing paused while Dawn explained, "This is my friend Pam Wilson. She chipped in to help with closing cleanup since Stacey's out. Pam, do you remember Nancy? We all went to Mimosa High around the same time."

Pam stifled a groan. *Nancy Warner?* Pam hadn't recognized her at first because the always thin girl had lost even more weight—the only plumpness on her entire body was in her shiny lips. The two women had never been in the same grade, but Pam knew exactly who Nancy Warner was, a former cheerleader with a wicked crush on Nick. Even though Pam hadn't stolen her boyfriend from anyone, she'd already been the indirect recipient of Nancy's hostility. Rumors had run rampant one month that Mae was sleeping with Nancy's still-married father. The Warners had divorced a year later.

From the way Nancy's unnaturally violet blue eyes narrowed, she definitely remembered Pam. "Wow, is that you, Pamela Jo? Goodness, what a surprise. We haven't seen you around these parts since… Let me think. Well, I guess not since you left your husband and baby."

Behind them, Dawn sucked in her breath in a sharp gasp, but didn't say anything. Probably because she was too stunned. Everyone froze, including the other stylist in the room and her client. The jilted redhead in the chair actually stopped sniffling, her mouth falling open as she was temporarily distracted by someone else's problems.

"That's right," Pam said mildly. "This is my first return visit since then." She continued to smile pleasantly and left it at that.

If Nancy was hoping for a catfight, she was going to be sorely disappointed.

But the woman took another stab at baiting her. "Alert the media! The *Monitor* should post an adultery warning. 'Be advised, there's a home-wrecking Wilson in town.'"

Mention of infidelity must have hit too close to home for the newly shorn redhead because she started sobbing again. The girl's beautician sent a scathing glare in Nancy's direction, mouthing, *Thanks a lot.* Pam decided this would be a good time to return the broom to the closet—a space bigger than most of the rooms at her house. Perhaps she'd stay there and thumb through old fashion magazines until tensions had lessened.

Next to the coatrack against the closet wall was a tiny table boasting a coffeemaker and a couple of folding chairs. Pam slid into one of them, unsurprised to see that Dawn had followed her.

"You okay?" her friend asked, looking miserable.

Pam nodded. "There's bad history between her family and mine. And it's not like she was wrong. I did leave Nick and Faith."

Dawn shifted her weight from one foot to the other. "Yeah, but that's none of her business. I'm sure you had your reasons."

Fragments came back to her—pretending not to hear the baby crying so that someone else would get her, the disjointed thoughts she'd had after they'd brought the baby home from the hospital. It was funny because, even though she hadn't had a drop to drink during her pregnancy or in the weeks after Faith was born, Pam recalled that postpartum phase much the way she did her worst benders. Blurry, shame-inducing snippets that felt more like bad dreams than reality.

"I wasn't a good mother. I decided Faith would be better off without me." And from what she'd seen yesterday, she'd made the right call. "Look, Dawn, you've been very sweet, but you don't have to do my hair. I've had a he… Heck of a day, and it sounds like you have, too."

"No, don't go! You can't let Nancy run you off just because she clearly has PMS."

Pam laughed despite herself.

"See, being around me has cheered you up already," Dawn said. "I'm delightful company—

ask anyone. So quit hiding in the closet and get your butt out there. I think our last official client is finished and paying as we speak."

"The redhead? There's someone who looks like she's having a bad day," Pam said sympathetically.

Dawn blew out a breath. "That girl is gonna hate herself tomorrow. She's worn her hair long for *years*. I've told Maxine, C-3's owner, when it comes to radical changes, we should have some kind of mandatory waiting period like they have for guns. Especially for any woman who's just been done wrong by a man."

Pam laughed again. It felt good. "All right, I give—you are delightful. I guess I'll stick around for that haircut."

"You won't be sorry. Wait until the shampoo! I give a very relaxing scalp massage. Have you ever thought about maybe changing your color a little, too?" Dawn asked. "Nothing radical, just some subtle lowlights to give the blond more depth."

Why not? If Pam was going to continue dealing with complicated mixed emotions and her newly acquired money pit, she might as well look good while she did so. *Never underestimate the power of a good hair day.*

"All right, show me to your booth."

While Dawn wrapped sections of Pam's hair in foil, Nancy finished her share of the cleaning and stormed out, taking the tension with her.

"Whew!" The stylist who'd been working on Red let out a low whistle. "I know Nancy's not always Little Miss Sunshine, but that was extreme." She met Pam's eyes in the mirror. "I'm Beth. And I'm guessing you must be the Wicked Witch of the West?"

Pam's lips quirked. "Something like that."

Beth nodded. "Which would explain your familiarity with the broom. You want a regular job sweeping up? We could sell ringside seats for the locals to come watch the fireworks between you and Nancy."

Considering the number of people in town who no doubt shared Nancy's opinions of Pam and her late mother, that idea sounded like hell.

Dawn painted another strand of hair and expertly rolled it up, the aluminum crinkling as she went. "Actually, Beth, people probably *would* turn out in droves to see Pam. But not because of any crazy grudge Nancy has. Pam was a real live TV star!"

"*Star* is too strong a word," Pam protested. "Even *personality* would be a stretch."

Dawn clucked her tongue. "Well, I watched

you every single week while you were on, and you were way better than that girl who took your spot when you left...or anyone else they had after. In fact, I think losing you was why *Country Countdown* stopped airing on that channel!" She stopped what she was doing, tilting her head to the side. "Speaking of careers, Beth may be on to something. Would you have any interest in some part-time work at the salon? Only temporarily, of course."

Nancy would hate the idea. "We already established that I don't have any cosmetology credentials," Pam said diplomatically.

"That's okay, we can't hire another stylist full-time and still hold Stacey's spot for her. With her being pregnant, she'd already cut back to a minimum of select customers. She didn't need to be working directly with chemicals and couldn't stand on her feet all day. So she was doing receptionist stuff—taking payments, answering phones, scheduling—along with just a few appointments and some light housekeeping."

Beth was nodding enthusiastically. "Like sweeping up the stations and doing laundry. None of it's too difficult, but it's hard for us to keep up with that stuff when we're already down a stylist."

"Especially since she won't be back until

after the baby!" Dawn added. "We weren't expecting her to be gone so soon. I'll bet Maxine would appreciate the extra manpower to help us transition."

Pam knew that Dawn was just trying to help an old friend and didn't even have the owner's authorization to make such an offer. Still, it was nice to be wanted for something, to be thought of as useful and competent—the mirror opposite of how she'd felt all morning while pieces of her former home fell down around her. "Thanks for asking me, but I am going to be swamped trying to remodel that house."

Then again, she did need to finance the remodeling.

And she'd certainly taken worse jobs before, notably a waitressing gig at a truck stop just off the interstate. If she could survive that, she could manage some dirty looks from Nancy Warner. Now that the other woman had vented, she would probably give up trying to rile Pam and simply ignore her. Pam's aunt and uncle had assured her that they were glad to help, but she was a grown woman. She didn't want to feel like a teenager who had to come to them for her allowance. Besides, they weren't made of money, no matter how successful Uncle Ed said his wife's jewelry-making had become.

Pam sighed. "So, this hypothetical job we're talking about—how much do you think it would pay?"

Chapter Nine

Faith shrank into the sofa, doing her best to disappear while Morgan and her mother argued in the adjacent kitchen. They were both yelling at top volume. It was so different here than at Faith's house.

On the flipside, at least Morgan had a mother.

Not that Morgan currently appreciated that blessing. "She is driving me *crazy,*" she complained once after her mom had stormed out of the house for an after-school meeting with the assistant principal. Morgan flopped dramatically into a beanbag chair, next to the coffee table where Faith had spread out their research articles. Ignoring their homework, Morgan continued her rant. "The assignment was creative writing, wasn't it? So I wrote a creative piece of fiction. *Fic-tion!* I'm not sure why everyone's making such a federal case out of it."

"Maybe because your story was too hot for a school assignment and sounded like it might be autobiographical?" Faith had actually been too squeamish to ask if any of it had been true. She didn't want to think about Morgan and Kyle like that. "If you don't want an uproar, don't be a pervert."

Morgan tossed her blond hair. "It was an artistic exercise."

"If you say so," Faith mumbled.

The two girls finally resumed work on their history project, a partner paper on the way fear had affected domestic race relations during World War II. Other student pairings had been assigned different periods throughout America's past.

After a few minutes, Morgan glanced up from her binder with a smug smile. "I'll tell you this. Mom is worked up enough about my short story that she actually called my dad. Do you know the last time they spoke that didn't involve lawyers? He's phoned every night this week *and* he's been answering my emails. Maybe that's what you need."

"A lawyer? Or email?" Faith frowned. "I don't follow."

"Honestly, Shepard." Morgan rolled her eyes. "You know I love you, but you can be so naive! You need an angle to get your mother to pay more attention to you."

"We should really focus on this project," Faith said. Her stomach hurt. "It's due in two days, and you spent more of this afternoon with your mom than me."

"Hey, this is me, your BFF! We can talk about this, right?"

"I guess so." But she'd rather not. For starters, Morgan kept insisting that her own mother and Faith's dad would be great together—*so not happening*—which made their conversations about Pam awkward. Mostly, though, Faith just didn't want to discuss the situation.

At first Faith had thought it would be enough to meet her mother. They'd never had a relationship before, so trying to force one now would be weird. Faith wasn't looking for anyone to French-braid her hair or read her stories. All she'd wanted was a few minutes to see the woman in person, have an actual memory of her. Once she had that, Faith had truly believed she would be at peace with the situation, content to have her dad.

But that had been before Pam took up residence in Mimosa! Word got around town fast, and Faith knew her mother had started working at the salon on Witherspoon. *So much for just passing through.* Growing up with no mother wasn't nearly as hard as not having a mom when the mom in question only lived a few blocks away!

What's wrong with me? Why doesn't she want anything to do with me? Maybe it was her dad's fault. There were obviously "issues" between him and Pam. Had he told Pam to stay away? Or was Pam simply not interested in getting to know her daughter? After all, Faith had spent her entire life in North Carolina and Mississippi, and she could be a little…bland. She wasn't as colorful as someone like Morgan. To a woman who'd traveled extensively, had lived in California and had even been on television, Faith must have seemed utterly boring.

"I screwed up," Faith muttered. "I'm so stupid."

"Don't say that! Half my grade depends on you." When her joking got no response, Morgan reached up to poke Faith in the shin. "Seriously, what's the deal, Shepard?"

"Pam asked me if I was interested in music. Like, professionally interested, and I told her I thought I'd rather work for NASA. Dumb! Music's one of the things I have in common with her. I should have, I don't know, pretended to think about it."

"That would have made a difference?"

"You said yourself, I need an angle. Music could have been it." Truth be told, Faith did love to sing. She just wasn't excited about the idea of doing so in front of crowds. What she really loved was writing her own songs, but she'd always been too embarrassed to show them to anyone. Maybe that was one of the reasons she liked Morgan—she admired her friend's fearlessness, even when it led her to make questionable choices. *At least she takes the risk.*

"It's not too late." Morgan rocked back, gradually getting to her feet. "You could still talk to her about music. You could talk to her about anything you want."

Faith snorted. "She hasn't been in contact with me since the one and only time we met."

"So?" Morgan grinned. "This is Mimosa. It's not like you don't know where to find her."

After her first full week on duty, Pam concluded that Beth the stylist had been right: there was nothing specifically difficult about Pam's new job. Her part at the salon required minimal talents—sweeping, answering the phone, cleaning equipment, shampooing customers. But she couldn't shake the feeling that none of those were the real reason Maxine had hired her. *I'm the sideshow freak.*

"Business has doubled since you've been here," Dawn whispered in between blowing steam off the top of her mug. The two of them were stealing a few moments' respite in the gi-normous storage closet that served as break room.

"Ah." Pam stirred vigorously. "So it's not just my imagination, then?" She used obscene amounts of sugar in her coffee, but she figured that, as far as vices went, that one was pretty innocuous. Life with Julia—who never met a sweetener she liked—was making Pam's habit even worse.

"You know," Dawn said sympathetically, "not everyone's here to gawk. Some people generally—"

"I realize the two of you are superbusy gabbing," Nancy announced from the doorway, enunciating her words so clearly that people down at Granny K's could probably make out what she was saying, "but there's someone out here who's specifically requested Pamela Jo."

"Coming," Pam called cheerfully. She enjoyed being cheerful to Nancy; it seemed to tick off the bitter woman. Dropping her voice, she turned to Dawn with a sigh. "You were saying, about how not everyone's coming to gawk?"

Dawn smiled sheepishly. "Look at it this way, most of the gawkers stick around as paying customers. You're like a one-woman boost to the local economy."

"I'll keep that in mind." Pam took one last sip of her coffee and poured the remainder into the sink. "Got a mint?"

"Sure." Dawn fished a plastic container out of her apron pocket, although if the person here to see Pam was only showing up to get good gossip, they probably deserved her rank coffee breath.

Nah. No one deserves that.

Pasting a cordial smile on her face and reminding herself of the latest batch of supplies she planned to purchase after work, she emerged into the main room of the salon. And found all eyes on her—some through surreptitious, sidelong glances, other gazes nakedly curious. Let them goggle, she didn't care. The only pair of eyes she was concerned with were the hazel ones staring back at her, filled with equal measures uncertainty and youthful bravado.

"Faith!"

The girl tucked her hair back behind her ear. "H-hi, Mom."

Pam flinched. "Don't call me that." *Not here, surrounded by these vultures.*

Cosmic irony. When Pam had been Faith's age, she hadn't want anyone to link her to Mae Wilson in public because she'd been embarrassed, felt she was better than her mother. Now Pam didn't want anyone to pay close attention to her relationship to Faith because the kid deserved better. Far better.

Rather than timidly retreat, Faith scowled, demonstrating a spark of temper. "Why not? You *are* my mother. Everyone in town knows it already. Pretending otherwise won't change anything."

"Fair enough." Pam didn't have much practice defusing angry tweens, but she figured proceeding with caution was her best bet. "How did you get here?" Mimosa was too small to sustain public transportation, but not so small that the girl could have walked to the salon from where she lived.

"Doesn't matter," Faith answered. "I just wanted to come say hello. And…and get my hair cut!" She tacked this last part on rather desperately, as if it were a spontaneous bid to keep Pam from sending her away.

Seeing the girl's vulnerability immediately after her anger made it all the more striking. Despite Faith's bravado, she was as fragile as Nick had worried she'd be when it came to her mother. Pam's heart tripped over itself, the beats erratic and her mood conflicted. She wasn't used to thinking of herself as a mother. She shied away from the title, knowing she hadn't earned it.

"You don't have to get a haircut," Pam said, wondering if her father gave her money for stuff like that or if she was dipping into her allowance, literally paying for the chance to spend a few minutes in Pam's company. That possibility caused another pang. "Come on. We can go for a walk or something."

If they stayed in the shaded parts along the sidewalk, it might even be a pleasant day for it. September was just around the corner, and some mornings there were hints of fall in the air. October and November were when it really started to turn pretty, with cooler breezes and colored leaves and—

With a start, Pam realized she would be gone before then. Surely even a handywoman with her inexperience could have the house in passable shape before October!

"I don't want to leave, I just got here," Faith

said mulishly. "I want to get my hair cut. I don't mind waiting my turn if everyone's busy."

What the girl obviously meant was *I want to spend time with you.* In a deep down, undisciplined part of her herself, Pam was thrilled, flattered that her daughter cared enough to seek her out. But panic was right behind—Pam knew from experience what happened when she gave in to her undisciplined, damn-the-consequences side.

Pam pondered her options. "All right. Stay then, but I'm taking that walk."

"Didn't you just get off your break?" Nancy whined, reminding Pam anew that no conversation with Faith would be private as long as they remained in the salon. "Our policy is one break in the afternoon and one in the morning."

Feeling more claustrophobic by the second, Pam whipped her head toward the reception counter where Maxine sat. "I'll be back in fifteen. If that's a violation of policy, fire me."

Maxine's eyebrows shot up, but there was amusement in her voice when she answered, "Oh, I don't think that'll be necessary."

It ended up being a more dramatic exit than Pam had intended when she first suggested to Faith that they go elsewhere. At least now the matrons of Mimosa had something to text about this afternoon. All Pam had really been trying to do was remove Faith from the situation so that the girl wasn't fodder for gossip. Pam was passing through—nearly anything was tolerable if it was only for a month—but this was Faith's *home*. The girl was entering her teen years, which would be hard enough without her mother's identity making her the object of speculation or ridicule.

Pam had acted out of a desire to protect her daughter but was left wondering if she'd done the wrong thing. Had she hurt Faith by walking away? *Little late to worry about that now.* Twelve years ago would have been the more appropriate time to second-guess that decision.

Fifteen minutes, as it turned out, were hard to kill. It wasn't long enough that she could truly get anywhere, like Granny K's to order some fries, but it was way too long for her to simply loiter in front of the salon. The way her day was going, the police would pick her up for looking like a suspicious character. *Can't say I'd blame them.* Salon dress code required all employees to wear black. On vivacious, curvy Dawn, her work smock looked like the Little Black Dress, reinterpreted for day wear. On greyhound-thin Nancy, the black added edge to her look, making her the neighborhood femme fatale. But Pam? Well, she was still too skinny and since she was cramming in as much renovation work as possible before and after salon shifts, her short, pale hair was often standing on end, accessorized with the occasional paint chip or handful of sawdust. Her build and coloring were not meant for the chic head-to-toe black—she looked like a cotton swab gone goth.

Only a few sidewalk squares from the burbling fountain where Pam sat, there was a tinkle of chimes, announcing the coming or going of a salon customer. Had Faith backed down and finally left? Pam glanced up hopefully but saw only a dark-haired woman who had considerably less gray showing in her hair now than when she had arrived two hours ago.

Pam turned away, hoping to discourage conversation. But the older woman trotted up to her and leaned against the fountain railing.

"I'm Martha," she said. "Want a licorice whip?"

Despite Pam's mood, she almost smiled. As hellos went, offering someone licorice seemed a bit random. "No, thank you."

The woman fished a resealable plastic bag out of her oversize purse. "My husband tried one of those patches when he gave up smoking a few years ago, worked like a charm. But not me. This is the only thing that's worked. Whenever

I get the craving, I have red licorice. Honestly I think it's been harder for me to quit smoking than it was to quit drinking."

Pam swiveled her head sharply toward the woman.

Martha smiled, keeping her voice low. "You don't recognize me, do you? I saw you at the last meeting, but I came in late and sat in the back. I won't intrude on your privacy, I just wanted to let you know…well, you're not alone. And I'm here if you ever need someone to talk to between get-togethers."

"Thank you." Pam was genuinely touched. This wasn't some passerby who had an over-developed curiosity about someone else's life, this was somebody who had been through it. "How long have you been sober?"

"Eight years."

"Wow." Even though Pam hoped to make it that far—fully *intended* to make it—the thought of all those days and weeks and months strung together, stretched in front of her… She swallowed, her throat dry and tight.

"I used to be a friend of your mother's," Martha added. "Well, social buddy anyway. I spent so much time at Wade's that I had my first wedding there! Guess it wasn't such a shock when that didn't work out. I'm remarried now. And I don't go down to the Watering Hole anymore."

"Good for you."

"Yes, it is. I won't say it's been easy, but it's been worth it. Keep that in mind for yourself, dear. I realize you're dealing with some difficult personalities—" she fluttered her fingers in the direction of the salon "—and probably some difficult personal situations. But hang in there. One day you could be the almost-to-a-decade nosy old lady butting into something that's none of her business."

Pam laughed. "I look forward to it."

After her chat with Martha, Pam's spirits were restored enough that she walked back into the salon with a smile on her face. She even managed to keep it there when she saw that Faith was in Nancy's chair and that the stylist was egging on the girl's rebellious moment. Her hair was a good six inches shorter! When the cut was finished, Pam watched Faith stare into the mirror, eyes wide as she considered what she'd done.

To keep her heart from sinking, Pam reminded herself that hair grew back. Eventually. Besides, maybe this would teach Faith to be more judicious with her actions. It wasn't even that the cut looked bad—if Nancy wasn't a stellar human being, she was still a decent stylist—but the new length was something of a shock. *She looks older.* Faith's features were highlighted differently. One no longer saw a pretty girl with a fall of long hair; one glimpsed the young woman she was on her way to becoming.

Pam had the oddest urge to give the girl a hug, feeling almost maternal in that split second. But she squashed the instinct. Pam could just imagine Nick's outrage if she encouraged Faith…and he'd be right. It wouldn't be fair to raise the girl's hopes that they could have a normal mother-daughter relationship. Not that Pam even knew what that was.

At the register, Pam took a collection of one- and five-dollar bills from the now subdued girl, the wad of cash making it clear that this was accumulated allowance. Nick would have simply handed her a twenty.

"Wait," Nancy called, "don't forget to apply the first-time customer discount. I've never cut her hair before." Since stylists liked to build their client base and end up with loyal, repeat business, it wasn't uncommon to use such discounts. But Pam suspected Nancy's offer came more out of guilt for taking the kid's money.

Pam handed back a five. "Here. Are you going to be able to get home okay?"

Faith rolled her eyes. "Got here just fine, didn't I?"

"About that. Faith, I work here. I'm sure you don't traipse onto your dad's construction sites in the middle of his projects. If there's an emergency, that's one thing, but…"

"Right. I get it. You don't want me around."

Yes, I do. More than I should. The girl's wounded expression triggered guilt so sharp that Pam swallowed, suddenly thirsty. She missed the days when she could have a drink to blunt the razor edges of unwanted emotion—but it had never only been one drink and the painful emotions had always been there when she was sober again.

If she couldn't make herself feel better, she could at least try to lessen the sting of her rejection for Faith's sake. "I don't want you at the salon," she clarified. "Not in the middle of my shift, anyway. It's unprofessional."

"But other times, when you're not at work?" Faith pressed. "Because there was something I wanted to talk to you about. Can you teach me to play guitar?"

Pam rubbed a hand against her temple, torn. It was so tempting, to seize the opportunity to spend more time with the girl. *Why doesn't she hate me?* That would almost be easier. "I'm only in town for a matter of weeks. Wouldn't you rather find a regular instructor who can keep working with you after I'm gone?"

Faith's shoulders hunched. "I guess. There's a guy my friend knows who might be able to help."

"There you go!" Pam smiled encouragingly. This other teacher would be for the best. Even though Pam periodically tuned her guitar, it had been a couple of years since she'd really played.

Faith didn't return the smile. Instead she glared as she pocketed her change. "See you around."

Pam watched the girl slink out of the salon, replaying her last words and wondering how literally Faith meant them. With most people "see you around" was a casual farewell. So how had her daughter managed to make it sound like a warning?

Although Pam didn't see Martha at Tuesday's meeting, there were other people who offered a friendly smile and word of welcome. After about twenty minutes, she decided she was comfortable enough to talk.

"Some of you knew my mother—she was hard

to miss. She was used to being a local legend—prom queen, Miss Mimosa in the town parade. But after that chapter of her life faded..." *After she had me.* "Her drinking became legendary. I started singing at an early age, and, looking back, I think part of the reason I pursued it aggressively was to manipulate the spotlight. I wanted every solo, every leading role in school musicals. Because the second anyone saw me, I wanted them to say 'You're that girl with the great voice,' instead of 'You're Mae Wilson's daughter.' I left town in the early days of things going bad for me. I've never been here as a failure before."

There'd been some scandal over her teenage pregnancy, but her peers had assumed she and Nick would marry anyway, so some found it romantic.

She jerked her thoughts from the past—from him—back to the present. "The spotlight's a lot less pleasant now, but even when people come into the salon and make a snide comment because they think they know my deep dark secrets, I remind myself that what they 'know' barely scratches the surface. The only person in this whole town who's ever seen me at my worst is me. And I'm determined never to see that woman in the mirror again. That's what keeps me from picking up a drink."

After Pam spoke, a married father of four talked about how he'd started drinking after being laid off two years ago. The ironic part was that he hadn't been able to stop drinking even when he did find new employment, ultimately costing himself that job, too. He was openly emotional while he spoke of letting his family down, and Pam could only imagine what it was like to be in his shoes. In some of her more self-pitying moments when she'd first joined AA, she'd told herself that she had it harder than most, trying to cope with her problems alone, no family to support her efforts. But she'd changed her perspective.

Jake, the family man currently trying to get through the probationary period of his latest job, had pressures she couldn't fathom. Any mistake he made affected the five other people in the world he loved most. There was a certain freedom in being alone. *Freedom...or cowardice?*

After the meeting broke up, Pam headed for her car, debating whether to go straight back to Aunt Julia and Uncle Ed's and call it a night or continue work on the floors at Mae's house. Pam had made a discovery last night—technically, very early this morning.

At first it had seemed as though the floors

were going to echo the walls. Beneath a peeling and unfinished layer of butt-ugly wallpaper, she'd excavated two more layers. When Pam had pulled up a mildewed corner of carpet, she'd found another layer of carpet and thought *here we go again*...but beneath that, hardwood! Honest to goodness hardwood floors. Sure, they weren't in pristine condition, but they were a far better alternative to the dingy carpet rotting atop them.

Did she have enough energy after almost no sleep the night before, a full shift at the salon, learning from Julia how to make a chicken pot-pie from scratch *and* a post-dinner AA meeting to drive back out to the house and finish liberating that floor? Imagining its full potential was almost enough to give her a renewed burst of energy.

Almost.

"Pam? Hey, Pam!" a male voice called from across the parking lot.

In some of the neighborhoods she'd lived previously, Pam wouldn't have slowed down in a parking lot at night to answer anyone. But the lot was brightly lit with old-fashioned wrought-iron lanterns and she was within both sight and earshot of a dozen or so other people.

"Yes?" She smiled expectantly, trying to remember the young man's name. When she'd spotted him in the meeting, she'd been taken aback; he didn't even look old enough to drink legally, although she supposed you didn't have to be able to purchase alcohol in a bar to develop a problem.

"I'm Richie," he said. "Two things. First, a couple of us missed dinner trying to get here on time from work, and we're going out for barbecue, if you'd like to join us. But also, I overheard you mentioning that you're trying to fix up the house your mom left you? I actually work in construction, for Bauer and Shepard."

She immediately had a visual of that company name on the side of Nick's truck—followed by the image of Nick getting out of the truck at her aunt's house, looking great in jeans as he strode purposefully toward her.

Oblivious to the fact that he'd lost half her attention, Richie continued. "I thought that if there are one or two projects you get stuck on, maybe some of us here can help you."

"Thank you, that's very kind of you to offer. I've already had dinner, but I might take you up on the—" Her phone, set to vibrate before the meeting, began buzzing around inside Pam's purse like a hive of angry bees.

She flashed Richie an apologetic smile. "Do

you mind? Very few people have this number, and it could be an emergency."

"Not at all." He waved, then caught up with his dinner companions.

She hit the answer button. "Hello?"

"Pamela Jo," Nick growled, "what in the *hell* did you do to my daughter?"

Chapter Ten

Pam rocked back on her heels. "Excuse me?"

"It's bad enough that I find out the two of you are meeting behind my back—didn't you respect me enough to discuss it with me? If you don't recognize my authority as a single parent, *you shouldn't have left her with me in the first place.*"

She was stunned, not only by the out-of-the-blue phone call but also by the depth of emotion in his words. How many years had he been waiting to lash out about that? On the other end of the phone, Nick fell quiet. Was he regretting his outburst or just biding his time until the next attack?

Making her way to her car, she gave him a moment to calm down. She slid into the driver's seat and locked her doors. "Nick, the only time I've seen Faith since that day you dropped her off was at the salon, where she just showed up for a haircut. I had no idea she was coming. She didn't even have an appointment."

More silence. Pam grew uneasy. He'd seemed upset about more than a single visit to the beauty shop.

When he finally spoke, his voice was softer, but tight, barely restrained. "She looks so much like you, now more than ever. She never wanted her hair short before."

Pam ran a hand self-consciously over her own short, spiky hair. "I didn't suggest she get it cut like that."

"You didn't have to. Don't you see that she—" He edited himself, changing tack. "But what about guitar lessons with that slimeball nineteen-year-old? She said that was your idea! That guy is bad news, and I don't want Faith within three miles of him, much less *alone* with him and *paying* to be there! You can't just waltz into her life—"

Pam's burble of laughter stopped him dead. *Oh, hell.* Where had that come from? There was nothing humorous about this call. Could she convince him it had simply been a nervous giggle and that she hadn't meant anything by it?

"My daughter's well-being is amusing to you?" he asked coldly.

"No, of course not. I…care about Faith, too. And I let her know when she came to the salon that I was worried about how she got there and how she was getting home. Even in a place as relatively predictable as Mimosa, she's too young to be gallivanting around alone and un-supervised." Too late, Pam realized that might sound like criticism of his parental skills, so she barreled onward. She'd rather he be angry with her for inappropriate laughter than argue with him about Faith.

"Okay, maybe one teensy thing struck me funny," she admitted. "Nick Shepard, protec-tive father? Vigilant against teenage guys with lustful thoughts! You're right to look out for her absolutely, but in my mind, I can still see *you* as that teenage guy with lustful thoughts."

"God, if any kid ever did to Faith what I did to you, I'd…"

Pam blinked. Was that self-recrimination she heard in his voice? "It's not like you had to se-duce me, Nick." She'd wanted him so much.

All through their first date, she'd wanted him to kiss her. It had escalated every time she was around him, staring into those blue eyes and breathing in that familiar cologne. Just the feeling of him coming up behind her in the library had sent tingles through her body. He hadn't even needed to touch her. Whenever he'd been close, she'd grown preoccupied with what it would be like when they touched later, when they were away from the school or when his parents weren't in view.

But she doubted telling him that, reminding him how hot they'd been for each other, was going to make him feel any calmer about raising a teenager daughter.

Nick cleared his throat. "You've really only seen her the once that I didn't know about, at the salon?"

"Of course."

"She made it sound like more. I wish I knew why. We've always been close, so why would she lie to me? Especially about something likely to make me angry. I thought kids lied when they were trying to cover their butts, not to get themselves into trouble."

Pam didn't have a simple answer for him, but she resented being used as a pawn in Faith's adolescent struggles with her father.

"I guess," he concluded, "she thought she could justify her actions by making them sound like her long-lost mother's idea, so she exaggerated the amount of time you've spent together. I've caught that friend of hers in situations like this. Since Morgan's parents are divorced, she feels like she can play them off each other with no one the wiser. It's hard for them to verify stories if they don't even speak to each other."

"Maybe," Pam said slowly, "we can nip this in the bud if we show Faith we are willing to talk to each other."

"Or willing to call each other screaming and hurling unfounded accusations?" he asked ruefully. "I don't normally yell like that."

"I'll cut you a break this once," she said, her tone light. While he'd definitely overreacted, these were extenuating circumstances. He was a single father staring down the barrel of the teenage years—that alone could periodically send a sane parent over the edge, much less a dad contending with his ex popping back into their lives after more than a decade. "Just don't let it happen again."

She'd learned to be a more forgiving person, but she wasn't a doormat. He didn't get a free pass to bite her head off whenever Faith frustrated him.

"You're one hundred percent right," he agreed. "This can't happen again, and I don't just mean my temper tantrum. We should show her, together, that she can't pull this crap. What are you doing tomorrow afternoon?"

Pam drove down Meadowberry, grinning as she passed Trudy's house. *I should stop by later and say hi.* The old woman would no doubt bluster as if Pam were interrupting something, but it was an act. Probably. Trudy had come into the salon two separate times since Pam started working there. The first to get her curls set, then a few days later for a manicure. And while Trudy had been as crusty as ever, not saying anything that could be considered warm directly to her erstwhile tenant, she was quick to cut Nancy off at the knees whenever the former cheerleader started in on Pam.

It was like having a knight to ride to her rescue. A misanthropic, senior-citizen knight who wore floral muumuus in place of armor.

Pam was still smiling over the image when she pulled into Nick's driveway. She'd agreed to meet him at his house for a late lunch. Then the two of them would confront Faith as soon as she got home from school. *It'll be an ambush,* Nick had predicted gleefully. At the relish in his voice, Pam had almost felt a twinge of pity for their duplicitous daughter.

She climbed out of her car, processing more of her surroundings. Her stomach fluttered with nerves. Everything was just so domestic—Shepard stenciled on the mailbox, Faith's bike chained up on the covered porch, a pair of muddy male boots by the front door. The house itself looked comfortable, nice without being pretentious or intimidating. A great place to raise a family and unlike any place she had ever lived.

Aunt Julia and Uncle Ed's home was a worthy attempt, she supposed, but smaller and cramped with fussy antiques that didn't encourage a person to kick back and relax.

Pam rang the doorbell, then forced herself to stand stock-still. She called on old drama discipline, the knowledge that she was visible on stage and couldn't fidget. But it took effort, hearing Nick's approaching footsteps on the other side of the door, not to fuss with her hair or smooth her navy skirt or pull at the loose thread she'd just noticed on the hem of her bronze top. Her clothes were rather lackluster today, but she'd felt the occasion called for something stern.

The door swung open, and Nick smiled at her. "Hey." And with that voice, those eyes, he could have been seventeen.

And she was seventeen again, too, her entire being lighting up at the sight of him. "Hi."

But then she blinked, and the faint lines that hadn't been around his eyes came into focus. He wore a black polo shirt that bore his company's logo, not a heather gray T-shirt that said Mimosa High Athletics.

"Thanks for coming," he said, ushering her inside. "It's decent of you to help me out, considering that Faith's sudden delinquent tendencies aren't your problem."

She tried not to be stung by the reminder that she wasn't a real part of Faith's life. Hadn't Pam told herself all along that was for the best?

"And considering the way I yelled at you over the phone," Nick added, his expression twisting in momentary self-disgust. "It won't happen again. Faith's a bright kid. If we want her to take us seriously as a united front, we can't be at each other's throats behind the scenes. Truce— for her sake?"

Pam nodded, knowing full well all the reasons he had to be angry with her and grateful that he was taking the high road. Unfortunately, declaring a cease-fire didn't automatically dispel the tension. She cast about for safe conservation.

"Something smells wonderful."

"Thanks. Gwendolyn's soup recipe, in the

slow-cook pot. I thought we'd have some salad with it."

"Sounds good to me." She set her purse down next to a decorative umbrella stand that seemed like a female purchase rather than something a man would think to buy. As she followed him toward the kitchen, she noted a half-dozen more ornamental touches that seemed feminine in nature. His mom, his sister? Or were these things left over from his marriage to Jenna? At the sight of a whimsical throw pillow featuring a unicorn at a waterfall, she added Faith to her list of potential decorators.

The kitchen was fabulous, full of light and open space and built-in shelves stocked with simple but top-of-the-line equipment. She made an involuntary whimpering noise. "No way will the kitchen at Mae's house ever look like this. I don't care how long people worked on it. The chefs at Le Cordon Bleu could consult on the kitchen design, and it would still be a nightmare."

Nick chuckled. "A nightmare? Guess I won't ask how the renovations are going."

She scowled. "Let's not speak of it."

He lifted the glass lid on the slow-cooker and stirred the soup, wafting the warm, rich smells of cumin and garlic and peppers through the room.

"Mmm." She breathed in deeply. "One of these days, I've got to take up cooking. It's a hobby, sort of, but only as a spectator sport. Most of the shows I watch now are food-related." She loved them, but tried to skip over episodes where they focused on the perfect wine pairings and cocktails to complement each dish.

"Yeah? Same here," Nick admitted with a grin. "My favorites are the ones where they travel somewhere exotic and try local cuisine. About the most exotic place I ever made it to was Destin, Florida. Faith and I vacationed at the beach for a few days."

That was a shame. Although Nick seemed reasonably content with his life—disastrous choices in wives aside—she remembered all the places they'd talked about seeing together. If she hadn't been pregnant, curtailing his college football plans, where would he be today?

Nick shook his head. "Who knows? Maybe one day I'll take Faith to France. But you... Seen a lot of places?"

"I've seen a lot of the exact same places in a lot of different cities. No matter where I was, it all started to feel alike." She'd been unhappy and jaded. At fifteen, she would have sworn that merely setting foot in Nashville or Hollywood would make her euphoric. But that had been a kid's dreams, bearing no resemblance to reality.

She'd learned the hard way that you couldn't just go to a new place and find joy there, not if you brought misery and guilt with you.

Changing the subject, she gestured at the produce laid out on the kitchen island. "What can I do to help?"

He set her to work washing and tearing romaine leaves at the sink while he chopped vegetables behind her. The steady rhythm was lulling, as was the simple, companionable silence between them. It wasn't until she noticed the strange limpness in her frame—her body unexpectedly relaxing—that she realized how much tension she'd been carrying lately. With golden afternoon sun streaming through the window and the comforting aroma of homemade soup curling around them, she felt far more mellow than she had since setting foot in Mimosa. This was why many people drank, she mused. That first glass of wine or sip of rich liquor? This warm, calm sensation, as if the soul had just breathed a contented sigh, was what people wanted to duplicate.

Nick broke into her thoughts. "Not that it's any of my business, but if the house renovations are so hellish, have you considered not doing them? Not doing them yourself, I mean. It might be worth it to hand the job over to a professional."

"You know any who work for free?"

"Ah, so it's a financial issue. It's possible, if Ed and Julia were willing to co-sign, that you might be able to get a small improvement loan against the projected sale price. Although loans aren't as easy to secure as they used to be in Mimosa."

Was this all off the top of his head, or had he given her predicament some thought? No doubt he'd made the logical deduction that the sooner the house was taken care of, the sooner she would get the hell out of Dodge.

She brought him the freshly washed leaves to be tossed with diced cucumbers, avocados and tomatoes. "My sticking with the house instead of dumping the whole mess on someone else isn't just about the money. It's also cathartic. I'm never going to get the chance…"

Her throat closed around a lump of emotion, Mae's face flashing in her memory. That was the downside of relaxing—you lowered your guard. In this domestic setting, her mother's death hit her anew. Pam would never share a peaceful moment with Mae as the two of them prepared a meal and simply chatted.

She swallowed, embarrassed that her vision was suddenly blurred and hoping Nick didn't notice her glistening eyes. "I'll never get to repair my relationship with her. Repairing the house is as close as I can get."

Nick brushed her cheek with the back of his knuckles. The gentleness of the gesture made her eyes and throat burn all the worse. "She loved you," he said quietly. "I don't know if it helps, after everything that happened, to believe that, but she did."

Pam bit the inside of her cheek. Despite what filmmakers and greeting card companies would have an audience think, maybe there were some things love couldn't overcome.

"Can I make a suggestion?" he asked, his voice still feather-soft. The tenderness was too familiar, bringing to mind so many past conversations and caresses. Her skin heated and she tried not to breathe in how good he smelled.

"S-sure." Pam made herself focus on his words rather than his nearness. "But if it's good advice, I can't promise I'll take it. That's not always been my strong point."

His lips quirked in homage to a smile, but his blue eyes were serious. "You sound like you regret the missed opportunities with your mother. And you're right, it's too late to do anything about them. So maybe keep your eyes open for future opportunities with other people."

Like you? She wanted to ask. *Like Faith?* She was here now, wasn't she? She was taking the opportunity—she just wasn't sure how far to take it. At what fork in the road did courageous wisdom become risky stupidity? Her gaze held his, broadcasting the questions she was afraid to put into words.

But apparently Nick didn't have the answers, either.

Stepping back, he cleared his throat. "We should eat. You can't properly reprimand a sullen tween on an empty stomach. Eating at the counter okay with you, or should we be fancy and have lunch at the table?"

"In the last week, I've eaten half my meals either in the storage closet at a salon or sitting on an upturned crate in a living room that's between floor treatments. The counter is plenty fancy for me. Actually, it might be too fancy. I'd feel more at home if we put a plastic drop cloth down and scattered some sawdust."

He laughed, and she grinned back at him, relieved at the lighter mood. As long as they stayed away from combustible topics like Faith and Mae, she was free to concentrate on a tasty lunch and undemanding conversation. They chatted about their favorite reality cooking show and who they thought should win. Eventually they even got brave enough to skirt the past and discuss people they'd gone to school with. Nick filled her in on details of who had ended up where, from those still in Mimosa to one who'd joined the military and was, as far as anyone had last heard, living in Alaska.

"I think I'd like to live in the north," Pam mused, "where there's snow. Sunny L.A. was not for me. I'd rather be somewhere cozy, wearing lots of sweaters and eating lots of soup."

Nick grinned at her. "They don't have soup in California?"

She rolled her eyes, not dignifying his smart-ass comment with a response.

"So that's the plan?" he asked. "To trek to the great white north after you leave Mimosa?"

"No firm plan." That was an understatement—she barely had a gelatinous plan. "I'm taking things one day at a time. Occasionally one hour at a time. Speaking of which, shouldn't Faith be home from school about now?"

He followed her gaze to the clock above the stove. "Whoa, I didn't realize it was so late." He bounced off his seat, grabbing his empty plate and bowl as he went.

She slid down off her own stool and carried her dishes around the counter to deposit in the sink. "Thanks for lunch. Your culinary skills have improved a lot since you took me on that picnic where you made peanut butter sandwiches."

He laughed. "You mean that time when I was in such a hurry to get you alone that I forgot the jelly and the drinks? Not my finest hour." Peanut butter on plain bread, with nothing to wash it down. "Tell you what, maybe I can make it up to you sometime. Cook you dinner?"

She blinked, dozens of questions fizzing to the top of her head like a carbonated soda someone had dropped before opening. Before she had a chance to articulate any of them—he didn't mean as a date, did he? With Faith or just the two of them? Did his willingness to spend time with her mean he'd forgiven her? She heard the front door open and shut.

"Hello? Dad? I saw the truck outside."

Nick and Pam exchanged glances. Showtime. As of this moment, they were a parental team, not to be taken lightly or easily divided and conquered.

"We're in here," Nick called. Would Faith notice the subtle way he'd stressed *we?* Would she have recognized Pam's car in the driveway?

Faith clacked into the kitchen in a pair of

stylishly heeled boots. She looked startled but excited when she spotted Pam. "Hi! What are you doing here?"

"I invited her," Nick said in his Grim Father voice. Pam knew instinctively that Faith would be hearing that tone again the first time she ever broke curfew or got a ding in the family car. "Because I think the three of us need to talk."

"I agree," Pam added quickly, not wanting Nick to come out of this looking like the bad guy.

"Oookay. Can I, like, get a soda first and sit down, or do we have to all stand here being weird about it?"

Nick jerked his thumb toward the living room. "In there. Now."

By unspoken consent, Nick and Pam took the larger sofa, leaving Faith the matching love seat on the facing wall. As she studied them, Faith raised a hand next to her face—looked confused for a second—then dropped it. The longer Pam watched her, the more she agreed with Nick's assessment from last night: *she does look more like me now.* The biggest differences between them were age and Pam's hair being far lighter.

Nick steepled his fingers under his chin,

affecting a look that suggested his ancestors might have been Inquisitors. Pam bit the inside of her cheek to suppress a highly inappropriate giggle. This stern disciplinarian was a guy who'd once been in on the plot to "borrow" a rival team's mascot.

"When I came home early yesterday," Nick began, "and found you here alone with a boy, which you know is completely against the rules—"

"He's *nineteen,*" Faith interrupted. "More man than boy. And I told you, he's a teacher. It's not like I'm dating him, Dad."

From the way Nick's jaw clenched, it was easy to tell Faith wasn't helping her case. "We'll get back to the advisability of you being alone in the house with a nineteen-year-old later," he promised. "But the part where you hired him, without talking to me about it first, as a teacher? Whose idea did you say that was again?"

Faith squirmed but glared at Pam, not ready to back down just yet. "I told you at the salon that my friend knew a guy, and you said it was a great idea. You said I should go for it."

"Ah," Nick said. "So it was your idea initially, not Pam's. And how about the way you made it sound as if the two of you had been regularly corresponding? How many times have you actually seen or talked to her?"

"Three."

"Not counting today or that day you met for milk shakes," Nick added.

The girl's gaze dropped. "Once." Her mumble was barely audible.

"And that's when you ambushed her at work?" he persisted.

In lieu of an actual answer, Faith crossed her arms over her chest and huffed out an aggrieved sigh.

Pam decided it was time for her to wade into the conversation. "Faith, you've made it seem like you want us to be…friends. But friends don't screw each other over. Why did you try to get your dad angry with me?"

"It wouldn't have happened if you'd taught me to play guitar like I asked," Faith accused her. "But you told me to get a regular teacher, one who wouldn't ditch me at the first opportunity."

As it turned out, working with Nancy Warner was fantastic practice for dealing with an angry young woman. "I did tell you to find a regular teacher," Pam agreed mildly, "but you're an intelligent girl and you know full well that I didn't mean you should find someone your father disapproved of behind his back."

"You never even mentioned wanting guitar lessons," Nick pointed out. "Yesterday was the first I've heard of it."

"You know I write my own songs," Faith said, picking at one of her cuticles. "I love music. Guess I inherited that from her."

The way she said it made Pam think it was a deliberate attempt to pit the two of them against Nick. Reflexively she reached out and put her hand atop his, making sure he knew they were in this together. "Your dad's a reasonable man, and you are his pride and joy. I'm sure that if you'd discussed this with him in a rational manner, letting him know guitar was important to you, he would have been open to the idea. But did you also know he has a helluva temper? You should have heard him when he called last night."

Faith had the grace to look abashed. "I didn't mean for him to take it out on you. Not really."

Pam waved her free hand dismissively. "That wasn't my point. I'm a big girl, and your father has already apologized. My point was that if you mess up and antagonize him and generally act like a bratty prima donna, you're going to lose your chance to do things you really want. And you'll only have yourself to blame."

Nick nodded. "Couldn't have said it better myself. Next week, you and I can talk about the guitar thing again. But I promise that if you do get lessons, it will be through an adult teacher I help select. Not some rocker bad-boy wanna-be your friend Morgan knows. In the meantime, you're grounded."

"Again?" Faith wailed. "I just got ungrounded."

"Make better choices," Nick advised calmly, "and maybe you'll stay ungrounded. As for Pam, don't stalk her. She has a right to go about her daily life without worrying about you showing up and making trouble."

"She's my mom," Faith argued. "I'm not allowed to go anywhere near her? Do you two even know how freakishly unfair that is? Other kids don't have to make hair appointments just to say hi to their mothers."

Pam's heart caught. Faith might be acting like a melodramatic tween, but nothing she said was untrue. *I need to get out of Mimosa as soon as possible.* It seemed that her staying here was having a negative impact on Faith. "I'm sorry this is hard on you—"

"Those are just words!" Faith said, eyes blazing. "If you were truly sorry, you'd see me. Talk to me, teach me guitar, take me shopping, ask about my homework. If you really felt bad about any of this, you'd be a mother!" With that, she raced out of the room.

Tears in her eyes, Pam sat rooted to the sofa. She didn't even realize she was still holding Nick's hand until he squeezed it. She was half-afraid to look at him, aware that she might find everything Faith had just said echoed in his gaze. Instead, when she chanced a glimpse at him, it was to find him watching her with a sad smile.

"Well," he said, "I guess we can agree she got my temper."

Faith knew that being grounded meant no phone, too, but she couldn't help herself. She called Morgan anyway. She figured her dad would be too busy talking to Pam for a while—they'd looked pretty cozy down there together—to check up on Faith.

"Yo, Shepard," Morgan said as soon as she picked up the phone.

"My father is so unfair!" Faith announced. "I'm grounded again."

"What class did you skip this time? And why wasn't I invited?"

"It's not funny, Morg. This is because of him finding me here with Rock yesterday. He went completely off the rails. He even called and yelled at Pam. She came over today so that they could both lecture me."

"Sucks," Morgan commiserated. For a girl who'd tested into advanced English, she was often a person of few words. "Sounds like the convos I used to have with my parents, back when they'd consent to be in the same room with each other."

"You think?" Faith hadn't really thought of it that way. She'd been so put out over the colossal injustice that her father could go see Pam without even telling his daughter that her mom was in town and that, judging by the two glasses at the counter and the dishes in the sink, it was okay for the two of them to have lunch together, but Faith was supposed to stay away from her mother.

The way Morgan put it was better. It almost made what happened this afternoon sound like a family moment.

Faith chewed on her lower lip. If she got herself in more trouble, would the three of them spend even more time together? Maybe they could even do some kind of family counseling. Would it be enough to keep Pam in town longer?

Bad idea. Faith shook herself out of the fantasy. If she wasn't careful, she could chase Pam out of town. After all, Pam had been quick to leave her behind before, and that time Faith hadn't even done anything—other than cry and poop or whatever, but all babies did that. If Faith was a brat, she might cause her mother to bolt.

Besides, she was sick of being grounded. Especially if there was a chance Bryce Watkins was going to ask her to the middle school's big fall dance. Homecoming might officially be for the high school, but all of Mimosa celebrated.

Maybe she should switch tactics, be the model daughter and student. If she did that, her dad and Pam might agree to let Pam take her dress shopping for the dance.

Assuming she's even still around. Her mother had always been very clear that she wasn't moving back to Mimosa. Why would she? She'd lived in far more exciting places—heck, she'd been on television! If her family hadn't been enough to keep her here when she'd actually been married to Nick, it was insane to think she'd choose Mimosa now. Part of Faith wanted to plead the case for Pam to stay, but her stomach roiled at the thought of being rejected. It was one thing to grow up without a mom and accept that as your norm. It would be far worse to be told you're unwanted.

"Thanks for letting me vent," Faith told her friend. "I should go before he catches me on the phone."

"Sure, anytime. You know I'm here for you, girl."

"I know." And she appreciated it. But calling to bitch to Morg wasn't the same as having a bona fide family.

Chapter Eleven

Since Pam had the day off from the salon, she'd planned to go to the house and work on renovations after leaving Nick's. She headed to Aunt Julia's to change her clothes, but ended up sitting on the foot of her bed, lacking the motivation to get moving. Even though she knew rationally that part of what she'd witnessed from Faith was over-the-top drama, a sign of the girl's age, some of the pain she'd seen had been real. *And I caused it.* Either by leaving in the first place or by coming back.

"Well, hello there," Julia said from the doorway. "I didn't realize you were home."

"I swung by to change clothes, with plans

to work on the house tonight." Pam spread her hands. "You can see how far I got."

Julia clucked her tongue. "You've been out there so much that we hardly see you. Why not take the afternoon off? I was going to run into town. We could make it a girls' trip—hit the craft store and stop for high tea."

Pam grinned. "High tea in Mimosa?" The local cafés sold more fried pickles than scones.

"You just have to know where to look. Come with me?"

What had Nick said earlier? *You sound like you regret the missed opportunities with your mother. So maybe keep your eyes open for future opportunities with other people.* "I'm in."

Her aunt clapped her hands together. "Wonderful! Let me go put my face on." That consisted of penciling in darker eyebrows and applying lipstick. Then she announced that she was ready.

Pam got into the passenger seat of her aunt's car, grateful not to be driving. She lacked the mental energy.

"Are you all right, dear?" Julia asked. "I don't mean to sound insulting, but, well, you've looked better."

"I've felt better." Pam studied her fingers on her lap, wondering where she should start. "You know that Nick came by your house once to see me? Faith, our…"

"I know who she is," Julia said quietly.

But Pam was determined to get the word out, to acknowledge her own child, even if the person who needed that acknowledgement most wasn't around to hear it. "Our daughter. My daughter. She wanted to meet me. We had what I thought was a very nice conversation over milk shakes one day, but it got more complicated after that. Nick asked me to come over today and talk to her. She's been having some discipline problems."

"Anything serious?" Julia asked, looking worried.

"Not yet. She's a good kid, just confused. And ticked off. I guess not having a mother will do that to you."

Julia mashed the brake harder than necessary at a stop sign and turned pointedly to her niece. "Some kids with mothers have it pretty rough, too, as I'm sure you recall." She didn't speak again until the car started rolling, her tone calmer and sounding more like herself. "Beating yourself up does neither you nor Faith any good."

Pam stared out the window, watching Mimosa pass by, noticing all the tiny, paradoxical ways that the town had both changed and stayed the same. "I know you're right, but there are times when it's hard not to beat myself up. This afternoon was draining, but it was only a couple of hours in my life. Nick goes through that every day. I wish things had been different for him, I wish I'd told him no when he asked me to marry him. If I'd had any sense at all, instead of torpedoing his college plans, I would have begged you and Uncle Ed to consider adopting Faith." She seemed to recall that her aunt and uncle had long ago tried to have children.

"We wanted to adopt you." Julia's words were so quiet that Pam thought she must have misheard them.

"What?"

Julia swallowed, keeping her gaze straight ahead, glued to the road. A rosy flush climbed her cheeks. "I've never been sure whether to tell you this. There's a chance you'll think I sound like a jealous, bitter shrew. But I think what scared me is that there's an equal chance you'll be mad at us for giving in and not trying harder."

"Aunt Julia, you and Ed have been wonderful to me since I came back to Mimosa. Nothing you say is going to change how thankful I am for both of you."

Sniffing, Julia turned onto a side road Pam

didn't recognize. "Ed and I tried to have children of our own. I got pregnant twice over the course of six years, and miscarried both times. And for her to…"

"Her, who? My mother?"

"I shouldn't speak ill of the dead. I don't want to tarnish whatever good memories you might have of her."

"All two of them?" Pam asked wryly. "I don't harbor any illusions that Mae was a saint. There were some times over the years when we laughed together or that she told me I was beautiful or that she surprised me with a home-cooked feast, but those weren't the norm. Whatever you have to say, go ahead and get it off your chest. Maybe we'll both feel better afterward."

"All right." Julia took a shaky breath. "Your mother didn't want you, at least not at first. She saw being pregnant as a burden. And I was incensed with rage that she would be so cavalier about the gift of life, especially knowing that I'd already lost one baby—the second miscarriage came later. Mae was always the life of the party, but the hard drinking and sleeping with other women's husbands didn't start until after your father left. She fell through a stained-glass window at a Christmas Eve celebration when you were four. It was then that I truly started to worry. Ed and I tried to help her, but it never worked."

"You can't help someone until they're ready," Pam said. "That's something I know personally."

"We reached the same conclusion, that we couldn't help her if she didn't want our help. But we thought maybe we could help you. When you were eight, you stayed after school for a special choir rehearsal and she forgot to pick you up. Nobody could find her, and the music teacher called me to come and get you. When Mae finally thought to come looking for you hours later, I was furious, even threatened not to give you over to her and she laughed! 'Why, Julia Lynn, that's kidnapping.' Ed and I scraped together money and consulted with a lawyer, but this was right after my second miscarriage. The legal advice was that we didn't have strong enough grounds for the state of Mississippi to separate a girl who hadn't been harmed from her rightful mother. We were also told that, in court, Mae's attorney would paint me as a grief-ridden, hormone-addled woman out to steal someone else's child because I couldn't have one of my own."

"Oh, Julia. That's awful." Pam heart squeezed

as she thought of what her aunt had been through. And then, after everything else the woman had endured, her teenage niece accidentally got pregnant. *Insult to injury—like mother, like daughter.* No wonder Julia had so often seemed bitter; she'd had cause to be.

"I should have fought harder," Julia lamented, "instead of leaving you with her. I was angry and ashamed. On some level, I was afraid the lawyer was right about me."

"He wasn't. You were trying to look out for me. The same way you're always trying to look out for Uncle Ed with that awful tea and the bacon that isn't really bacon," Pam teased gently.

Julia gave her a watery smile. "Thank you for understanding. I promise the place we're going has excellent tea and real clotted cream."

Considering Julia's confession in the car and Pam's draining encounter with Faith, tea could have been a dreary affair. Instead, it was charming. The Royal Cup was fanciful in its setup, as if the entire café was a little girl's dress-up tea party. Stuffed animals lined the shelves of one wall, and the china dishes were of high quality but all mismatched. Julia and Pam were offered a feathered boa and a sequined scarf upon arrival.

"Don't tell me you have a silly side," Pam muttered to her aunt.

"Nonsense. I only come here because of the antioxidants in the tea. Don't let's mention this to your uncle."

They had tea with actual cubed sugar and scones with cream and fruit. Considering what a wonderful time Pam was having, it was strange that her thoughts went in the direction they did.

"Julia, I was thinking that maybe, just for the time being, I'd move out to the house. But I wouldn't want to hurt your feelings. You and Ed have been so good to me!"

Her aunt set a rose pink cup down in its saucer. "This isn't because of anything we've said or done?"

"No, ma'am. Part of it is a convenience issue. I'm usually so tired by the time I finish at night, I might as well sleep at Mae's. But more than that, I want to prove to myself that I'm honestly making the place inhabitable. Of course, to actually inhabit it, I'll need some furniture basics. I suppose I *could* use a sleeping bag, but I'd rather not."

Julia waved a hand. "Your uncle runs a furniture showroom. We are not letting any niece of ours sleep on the ground, for heaven's sake. If you're sure this is what you want, we'll help."

"I'm sure." *I think.* "Oddly enough, feeling closer to you gives me the confidence to do it. If that makes sense."

"You feel closer, so you're ready to move farther away? No, dear, no sense whatsoever," her aunt said fondly. "We'll talk to Ed over dinner about some furniture options. And after this weekend's big jewelry show in Waycomber, my schedule slows down until the holiday craft fairs start up in November, so I'll be able to come over and help paint or wallpaper."

"Thank you. God knows I could use the assistance."

"Done, then."

Once they'd finished their tea, they progressed to a nearby craft store in much higher spirits. Julia said she needed more "crimp beads," which Pam gathered to be some sort of fasteners to keep stones in place so that a piece of jewelry hung properly. But no sooner did they get to the jewelry-making section of the store than Julia's shopping list exploded from one item to ten.

"We may be here a while, dear."

"No hurry," Pam said indulgently. "I think I might want to commission you to make a couple of things." Before she left town, she'd like to give presents to Trudy and Dawn. Maybe a necklace for the older woman and earrings for Dawn, something that wouldn't get in her way or catch on her smock buttons at the salon.

Julia made a little murmuring noise to show she was listening as she rounded an aisle, never lifting her gaze from a row of red stones that were so alike in hue and size that Pam had no idea how her aunt could tell them apart. Sometimes, watching her aunt work, she thought that Aunt Julia's hobby required vision and dexterity as precise as piloting a plane for the air force.

"Did you have specific colors in mind?" Julia asked. "Because if you do, we could get materials while we're here."

"No, I was mostly thinking out lou—" Pam stopped and nearly knocked into her aunt, who'd made another turn to investigate a rack of clearance inventory.

Right down the aisle from them stood Gwendolyn Shepard and one of her bridge club friends. The minute Gwendolyn saw them, she sucked in a breath, clearly affronted by Pam's presence in the store. Or on the planet.

"You." Gwendolyn's eyes were her son's, without any of the warmth. Her gaze was blue ice. "I heard you were in Mimosa, but I don't think I really let myself believe it. Deep down, I didn't think anyone would really be that brazen."

Suddenly Aunt Julia was standing between them, crimp beads and semiprecious stones forgotten as she faced down Nick's mother. "This town was Pamela Jo's home and she has family here, same as your son. She has every right to visit whenever she wants."

"Even if her being here is detrimental to an innocent child?" Gwendolyn demanded. She looked over Julia's shoulder, once again skewering Pam with the force of her contempt. "I hope you're happy! You've been here a matter of weeks, and already you've ruined that girl."

Ruined? *And I thought the twelve-year-old was melodramatic.*

"That terrible haircut," Gwendolyn sneered, taking in Pam's own short hair. "Ditching class, running around with inappropriate boys!"

"As inappropriate as your son was as a teenager?" Julia interjected with saccharine sweetness.

Wow. *You go, Aunt Julia.* Pam was shocked to hear her aunt stick up for her so forcefully. Still, the last thing she wanted was an over-fifty catfight in the craft store.

"Ladies, why don't we all agree to disagree and go our own separate ways?" she said. Would Nick tell his mother about this afternoon? No doubt Gwendolyn would add the blame for Faith's outburst atop Pam's other sins.

"Separate ways is a fine idea," Gwendolyn said. "Keep that in mind, and stay away from my granddaughter and my son."

"Nick's a grown man now," Julia said. "You can't control him anymore. Not that you did such a great job of it even when he lived under your roof."

With that Julia spun on her heel, and Pam quietly followed suit. They left the store without having bought anything. Once they'd reached the parking lot, Pam said, "Not that I don't appreciate your taking my side…but what you said wasn't particularly nice, Aunt Julia."

Her aunt glanced up sheepishly from the remote that unlocked the car. "You're right. But it was tremendously fun. Are you disappointed in me?"

Pam finally released the laughter that had been building ever since Julia had rendered Gwendolyn Shepard speechless. "Disappointed? If I ever win the lottery, I'm having a statue built in your honor. That was awesome!"

Julia smiled beatifically. "Drink more tea and eat less salt, dear, and we'll call it even."

Nick marveled at the unspoken family politics that allowed his brother-in-law, A.J., as man and wage earner, to sit in the living room and unwind while the women cleaned up, yet Nick—also a male breadwinner—was expected to help with the dishes. Not that he minded working in the kitchen. On the contrary, if he could get Leigh and his mother to go in the next room, the cleaning job would be downright peaceful.

Instead, his mother and sister were harping at him. Faith and her cousins were all upstairs doing homework. Nick was seriously willing to consider some night courses if it got him out of this customary, tag-team browbeating.

"I'm not saying that I have an opinion on her hair," Leigh explained defensively.

"Well, I do." Their mother shoved a baking sheet into a cabinet with a metallic clatter. "And I hate it."

"My point," Leigh continued, "was simply that the hair is a first step. She did it without your permission, Nicky. The next thing you know, it escalates. Getting her ears pierced without asking first."

"She already has pierced ears," Nick pointed out, not that either of the females he was related to listened. He'd agreed to let Faith have her ears pierced as her birthday gift for her tenth birthday. How could it seem like such a long time ago and yet also feel just like yesterday? Having a child seriously messed with the time-space continuum.

"Tattoos!" Leigh was saying. Apparently her parenting credo was "Today, Short Hair—Tomorrow, a Belly Ring and a Boyfriend Named Viper."

Nick banged a pot down on the counter, effectively catching both women's attention. "Knock it off," he said when he was certain they were listening. "For starters, Faith is scared of needles, so I think we can rule out tattoos." She'd gone so pale after her ear piercings that he'd worried she would pass out. Although, even if she did come home with a nose or belly-button ring, it wasn't as though he'd love her less.

"I'm proud of Faith," he said. "My biggest overall complaint about her behavior, quite frankly, is her tendency to overreact. And now I'm thinking she gets that from us, the adults in her life. Leigh, you might as well be running in circles shouting, 'The sky is falling.'"

His big sister sniffed. "That's a hell of a way for you to talk to me in my own home!"

"I doubt you would have taken it any better in anyone else's home," he said. "You have got to get a hobby, take up meditation, find some way to relax. Along the way, you seem to have forgotten how to breathe."

Leigh narrowed her eyes. "I breathe just fine, thanks."

Rather than get sucked into an intense argument about how easygoing his sister was, he turned to Gwendolyn. "And you! Your biggest goal in life seems to be keeping Faith away from Pam, but by demonizing her mother, you're not only potentially harming Faith, you're making her more curious and rebellious. When I talked to Pam about it—"

"You spoke to her?" Gwendolyn demanded. "Recently?"

"Two days ago. She came over for lunch. She loved your soup by the way."

Gwendolyn, a normally dignified woman who disliked anyone making a scene, looked nearly apoplectic. "I knew this would happen, I knew it! You've never been able to stay away from that woman, and this time is no different. Didn't I warn you?"

Nice to see they'd taken his comment about

not overreacting to heart. "It was just a quick lunch to talk about Faith, figure out a parenting strategy."

"She is not Faith's parent," Gwendolyn said in a low, dangerous voice. "Pardon my crudeness, but she was an incubator! She never cared for that girl. She didn't put bandages on scraped knees or teach her multiplication facts or sing her to sleep at night. We did all that. *We're* Faith's family! Pamela Jo Wilson is merely a bad influence. It's as I told her in the craft store—"

"You talked to Pam?" Nick was beyond affectionately annoyed now and moving into downright pissed.

"I didn't show up at her house in the dead of night," Gwendolyn snapped, "I merely ran into her while shopping."

"And were no doubt your charming self," Nick drawled sarcastically. He recalled all the subtle digs his mother had made over the years, the times he'd had to defend his girlfriend, "the daughter of that low-class Wilson woman," to his mother. He didn't think Gwendolyn was technically an evil person, but she was snobby and prejudiced when it came to anything involving her children.

What bothered him, remembering those many squabbles they'd had about Pam, was the way they'd suddenly stopped. *When we got married.* He'd been so shaken by the discovery that he was going to be a father, had felt so guilty and dependent on his folks, that he'd stopped voicing a dissenting opinion. He'd needed his mother and father to tell him everything would be all right, so he'd overlooked the less than warm reception they gave his bride. While Gwendolyn hadn't been expressly hateful, neither had she rolled out the welcome mat.

"Oh, Nick." Gwendolyn sat at one of the chairs around Leigh's kitchen table—Leigh always ate at her table; she was the good sibling. "I don't care whether I was charming to Pam when I saw her or not. What I care about is you and Faith. She needs to leave the both of you alone. I tried to appeal to her sense of decency, although that would assume she has one, and—"

"Mom, shut up."

"Nicholas!"

"I should have asked you to butt out thirteen years ago. If I had, maybe I'd still be married."

Gwendolyn's eyes doubled in size. She was spluttering inarticulately, unable to form a whole word.

Leigh stepped in on her behalf. "Surely you're not trying to blame us for what happened?"

"I blame all of us. Her, myself." Before the

baby came, when Pam had shut down emotionally, she'd tried to talk to him about his parents, the way their disapproval had chafed. But,
needing his family's support, he let himself believe she was exaggerating her pain. "You guys
weren't nice to her. She was a scared, teenage
girl who didn't have the benefit of coming from
a stable family like I did. You two have always
been so protective of me. If you'd extended even
a little of that to her, made her feel like one of
us, maybe…"

He clenched his fists together, wishing he
really could do things over again. "Or maybe
not. We'll never know now, will we? The past
is done. But this the present. And the two of
you. Will. Be. Nice." He felt like a comic strip
character, the words appearing in a dialogue
bubble over his head in all caps. "You're not
the mob. You don't get to make her disappear
or send her on a little drive."

"We love you." The way Leigh brandished
a rubber-tipped spatula at him as though she
might thwap him upside the head was at visual
odds with her words. "You can't honestly expect us to sit by and say nothing if we see you
making mistakes!"

"I love you, too," he told his sister, "and I
value your input. But that's what it has to be—

input, just something I take into consideration before making *my* final decisions. You two can't run my life, and I don't want you running people out of it. If you can't respect that, then maybe Faith and I need to think about settling somewhere other than Mimosa."

Gwendolyn made a strangled noise. Nick crossed the room to get her a glass of water out of the refrigerator's filtered faucet.

After she drank, she was composed enough to ask, "You'd really take my only granddaughter away from me?"

"Honestly?" He looked her in the eye. "I don't know. But I hope you won't push me so that we have to find out." He knew that his mother had been lonely since his dad died; the last thing he wanted was to remove even more family from her life. But this controlling, hateful side of her was the one aspect of her he couldn't tolerate. He'd done so for years, thinking that he was being a dutiful son, but now he had Faith to think about, too.

"I don't know if Pam will be staying in Mimosa much longer," he said, wishing the thought of her going didn't cause such a sharp twinge. "But we don't own the town. She has every right to be here, and Faith is actually hoping to be closer to her mother before she leaves. We will be supportive and nontoxic in our remarks. Agreed?"

Leigh shot him a look. He doubted he'd be invited back to dinner at his sister's anytime soon. And if he was, he was pretty sure she planned to spit in his food. But she nodded.

"Good. Thank you," he said. "Mom?"

"You've always had a blind spot when it came to that woman," Gwendolyn grumbled. "Now is no different. You're not even a couple anymore, and you'd choose her over family?"

"Mom, for a while, she was my family, and I made a mistake in *not* choosing her. Trust me, you're a better person than this."

"I'll be civil to her if I happen to see her," Gwendolyn vowed grudgingly. "And I won't speak an ill word of her in front of Faith. But the day Pamela Jo leaves town, I plan to dance a damn jig."

Well, it was a start anyway.

Chapter Twelve

When headlights flashed through the untreated windows at the front of the house, Pam assumed her aunt and uncle had forgotten something. After all, they'd only left about ten minutes ago. She went to the front door, which she'd locked behind them, and was surprised to glimpse Nick coming up the sidewalk. Her first panicked reaction at seeing him out here unannounced on a Friday night was that something must have happened to Faith. But logic kicked in as she was opening the door—in an emergency situation, it would have been quicker to simply call her.

Still, she couldn't help greeting him with, "Is everything okay? Faith, is she—"

"She's fine," he assured her. "She's at a slumber party at her friend Tasha's house. Of course, Morgan was invited, too, so they've probably all sneaked out and are merrily toilet-papering the neighborhood even as we speak." He swatted away a couple of moths that were drawn to the light spilling from the doorway. "Can I come in?"

Pam took a step back, giving him room.

He glanced around, his expression unreadable. "You're making progress."

"Thanks," she said shyly. She felt like a painter who'd had an unexpected visitor to the studio, viewing a potential masterpiece when it was only half-finished. Did Nick see the as yet unrealized charm in the place, or was his vision obscured by holes that still needed to be spackled in the walls and a naked lightbulb shining where she hadn't hung the new fixture?

Furnishings in the house were sparse but adequate. In the living room, she had a couch from her uncle's store and an Ole Miss beanbag chair. The closest she had to a table was a crate, but Uncle Ed was expecting a shipment of secondhand furniture from an estate sale next week; there might be something promising in that.

She didn't have a television, which wouldn't have done her any good, anyway. Although the electricity was on, as well as running water in all but the smaller bathroom at the end of the hall, there was no gas or cable right now. The only cooking she could do was in the microwave, but it would be November before anyone would need central heating out here.

A semi-stocked refrigerator hummed in the next room, Aunt Julia had given her a freestanding, antique linen wardrobe for towels and sheets, and in the main bedroom, there was a futon that pulled out into a queen-size bed. *Beats sleeping in my car.*

She gestured graciously toward the new sofa. "Have a seat. Want a bottle of water? Afraid I'm pretty limited in my refreshment options."

"No, thanks. I'm good. Did I catch you at a bad time? If you have a few minutes to take a break, I thought maybe we could talk." He patted the cushion next to him.

Pam's self-preservation instincts murmured that she should ignore the patting and take the beanbag chair, but that was ridiculous. She didn't want to sit at his feet, looking up at him like a child at story time, and there was plenty of room on the couch. She'd survived sitting right next to him in his living room the other day. *We were chaperoned then.*

They hadn't been alone in a dark house, in the exact room where they'd first made love. She brushed her hands over the denim cutoffs she wore, trying to dust away the memories with the grit. Staying as close to the opposite edge as possible, she sat with him.

"I probably don't smell so good," she said bluntly. "I've been working hard since two o'clock this afternoon."

Nick laughed. "You smell fine, but thanks for the warning."

Curiosity was eating at her. "If you're not here because of Faith," she wondered, "what was so important that you drove out after dark instead of just picking up the phone?"

"Because I thought what I had to say, you deserved to hear in person." He drew a deep breath. "I'm sorry."

She frowned. "Is this still about losing your temper on the phone earlier in the week? That's behind us."

"No, this is about our marriage."

Her eyebrows shot up. "You're sorry about our marriage?" Not that she blamed him—she'd be sorry if she married her, too—but she was still surprised that it had merited a middle-of-the-night visit.

"I'm sorry I screwed it up so badly and didn't do more to protect you. You have to understand, my mom loves me a lot. My dad did, too, so I got to see the occasional kinder, gentler sides of them. But I'm aware that she can be a dragon lady to people she…"

"Hates?" Pam suggested cheerfully.

"Doesn't understand, I was going to say."

He made it sound as if they were two small nations who'd suffered from cultural miscommunications. "Dude, I'm pretty sure she wanted me dead. If I hadn't been carrying her grandchild, she would have put a hit out on me."

Nick snickered but tried to cover it by running his hand over his face.

"This is one of those 'funny because it's true moments,' isn't it?" she asked drily.

"Well, it's just interesting that you should mention my mother in the context of a hit-man contract. I told her the other night that she had to stop acting like a mafia don."

"You did not." Pam tried to imagine Nick standing up to his mother; based on her experiences during their marriage, she couldn't do it. "To her face?"

He sobered, the traces of shared humor fading from his expression. "Yeah. And I should have done it years ago. This is my point, that I let her make my wife feel so unwanted in our family."

As Pam had done at his house during their talk with Faith, she reached out unthinkingly, squeezing his hand for moral support. But this time, he flipped his hand over, lacing his fingers between hers.

"You were just a kid," she said, absolving him. "You weren't ready for marriage and the politics of balancing between your wife and family, much less a baby on the way." Very subtly she tried to wiggle her fingers free. She supposed she could just yank out of his grasp—it wasn't as if he was going to hold her hand against her will—but she was hoping the withdraw might go unnoticed.

The knowing grin he gave her made it clear she wasn't nearly covert enough. He leaned even closer. "I know it's not fair to put you on the spot, all these years later, and play the what-if game, but I can't help it. If I'd stood up to my parents, showed you more clearly that you were loved, do you think you might have stayed?"

She wanted to squeeze her eyes shut against the hope in his gaze. It was like staring into the sun with a skull-splitting hangover. "No." She pulled her hand back, subtlety be damned. "I wouldn't have stayed, Nick. Nothing you could have done or said would have changed that, so you can let it go. You're absolved."

The hope vanished, replaced by irritation. "Explain it to me," he demanded. "After the years we had together, you owe me that much, Pam. I thought that, after all this time, it wouldn't matter anymore. Seeing you again, it does."

She stood, deciding brutal honesty was her best bet but not entirely sure how to articulate what had she'd gone through. "I don't know how well I can explain this. Hell, I don't even remember those months very clearly. Most of the time it was like I was sleepwalking, or like I *wanted* to be asleep. You were so cute with Faith, looked so happy when you were holding her, and I just… Annabel and I talked about this a lot last year. I did some research on postpartum depression. Statistics indicate that it's more common and more severe in teenage mothers."

Nick nodded. "I thought of that. Not at the time, but later. One of the guys who works for me, his wife, Lisa, had twins and she had trouble with PPD after they were born. They missed the signs at first, assuming it was just the understandable fatigue of dealing with two newborns. But after it got worse, they talked to a doctor. If that's why you left...how come you never came back?"

He rose, too, and paced back and forth across the small room. "After you'd been gone a few months, I got scared to death. Despite the note, I was convinced you wouldn't have stayed away from us that long. I thought..." He swallowed, shaking his head. "I thought something had happened to you. And when you popped up on that cable show? I hated you so damn much. Two and a half years of worry replaced with the realization that while I was trying to potty train Faith and roofing out in the hot sun for Donald Bauer, you were hobnobbing with country music stars and going to work every day at a television studio."

"I should have sent you a letter telling you I was okay."

"You think?" His voice was level, but old embers of banked fury still glowed within him.

She couldn't stand for him to think she would have blown off her husband and baby to go play guitar. She had to make him understand.

"I told you that most of it's a blur," Pam said. "But there's one day I remember. She was crying—which could have been any day. Whenever I was with her, she was crying. She smiled at you, even your mom, but I think she sensed the tension in me. Anyway, she was shrieking because she had a rash and had done something toxic in her diaper. I was trying to change her, and I was making a mess. She just kept kicking, and I couldn't get her clean. I heard myself yell, 'You're ruining my life' and it was Mae's voice coming out of my mouth. I might... I'm so sorry, Nick—I might have even shaken her. Only for a moment, but long enough to be horrified at my behavior."

Pam pressed her fingertips to her eyes, belatedly aware that she was crying. Tears ran down her face, but she forced herself to keep going so that he could understand how truly awful she'd been. Maybe then he'd stop mourning the abrupt end of their marriage and just be glad Faith hadn't been subjected to her.

"It was an epiphany," she said. "I was going to be Mae. She'd raised a daughter she hadn't wanted in the first place. Even though she was a married adult when she got pregnant with me, she resented me my entire life, certainly never gave me a role model for loving maternal behavior. And even though I couldn't bond with Faith, couldn't love her, I knew for damn sure that I wanted better for her. I wouldn't wish my childhood, my mother, on anyone. So I got the hell out of there. And I feel like, with your questions tonight, you want me to say I'm sorry for what I did. But the thing is, I can't."

He understandably viewed her actions as desertion, but the other way to look at it was that she'd set them free. In a moment of piercing clarity, she'd embraced the truth Gwendolyn Shepard had made clear all along, that Nick would be far better off in the long run without her.

Did Nick see that now, that she'd done them all a favor? "Faith's had you, and even your dragon lady of a mother, and our daughter turned out... She's beautiful. Smart. A little bit of a pain in the ass, but that just means she's a normal kid so you've done your job right." Pam hiccupped, aware she was rambling hysterically, but Nick watched her, silent and dry-eyed, letting her get it all out. "I can't apologize for leaving the two of you. Because I knew in my bones that it was the right thing to do and the horrific mistakes I made after I left here prove that.

"Nick, you would have been so ashamed if you could have seen me. I was not someone you could have in good conscience let near your child. Even though I tried to run away from it, I still turned into Mae and every ugly thing I ever hated about her. Given the same set of circumstances, I'd leave you and Faith again." And maybe that was what she felt guiltiest about, above everything else. What kind of unnatural woman not only abandons her baby but can't even bring herself to regret it?

The tears were a torrent. "I... I could have hurt her if I'd stayed. I couldn't risk that, couldn't live with it." She buried her face in her hands, wishing that the crying could wash away the past, make her clean again.

Then suddenly Nick was there, tugging her clumsily into his arms and folding her against his chest. He was out of practice—he'd done this so many times before, whenever her mother said something awful. Or that day when Pam had found her mother passed out and had thought for a split second that Mae was dead.

She'd sobbed afterward because one of the feelings she'd experienced before panic kicked in had been relief. She'd trusted Nick enough to admit that to him, and he hadn't judged her. He'd just listened.

I've missed him so much. She looped her arms around his neck and leaned into him. The rhythm of his heartbeat steadied her, and as she calmed, her gratitude gave way to hypersensitivity. The plane of his chest was well-muscled from time spent in construction, hard beneath his shirt and against her body. He still used the same shampoo he always had, and she inhaled the familiar smell, letting the memory take her back. The soothing metronome of his pulse had picked up speed. She wasn't the only one reacting to their embrace.

His breathing grew rougher. "Pam."

She looked up reflexively, and his mouth took hers. Heat arced between them, invisible lightning that singed her in all the right places. The kiss quickly turned into a frantic homecoming, each of them desperate to touch and taste. There was nothing harmonious or well-orchestrated about their movements, simply raw feeling. They bumped noses and foreheads in their haste.

He backed her against the couch and they toppled together, landing in a pile of limbs and pleasure. Her breasts tingled beneath his weight, and she rocked her hips upward, denim scraping denim, to meet his. He was so hard it made her dizzy, imagining what they'd be like, the slide of him inside her.

She hooked one ankle behind his calf, pushing him against her, and he nipped her earlobe. His hands seemed to be in so many places at once. He cupped her under her shirt and the symphony of sensation overwhelmed her. Arching her back, she bit back a cry, marveling that she could be so close to the brink of orgasm. The desire she felt was so sharp it was uncomfortable.

Nick dragged his kisses downward, his lips closing around her nipple as he kept moving against her, the pressure maddening and demanding, and she broke, this time unable to keep herself from crying out as wave after wave rippled through her. Her body felt swollen and sensitized in the aftermath, and dazed, she tried to shove him away.

"I cannot believe I did that," she said to the ceiling, embarrassed. "That was…"

"Earth-shattering?" Nick flashed her an adorably cocky grin.

Out of control. She sat up, tugging her shirt and bra back into place. Letting her common sense get eclipsed by the moment was a bad idea for an addict. One kiss had turned into much more so fast her brain hadn't been able to process it. It was reminiscent of the way a single drink to help her loosen up before a show had once turned into a sloppy, intoxicated performance that had tanked the last of her professional credibility.

"That was too much," she said. "What happened to discipline?"

He reached for her, trying to joke away her tension. "I didn't know you were into the discipline stuff. Maybe next time."

"Nick! I'm serious. That…" She blinked. "I've had too many mindless one-night stands."

"We don't have to talk about that. Neither of us have been completely celibate, and I'm not going to hold your history against you."

"It's not about you holding anything against me, it's about me holding myself accountable. I don't want this anymore. I don't want you to be just a quick lay."

He flinched, then stood. "That kind of talk is kind of a mood killer, sweetheart."

Good. Because it would have felt too selfish to send him out of here still aroused while she was satisfied. *Sort of.* Her body might have just released months of tension, but she wasn't exactly giddy with afterglow. She wanted to curl into a ball and cry, which was what had landed her in this mess in the first place. Tears weren't the answer.

With a sigh, Nick resumed his pacing. "I don't mean to downplay what you've been through, but is there any chance you're over-reacting? Getting swept away with your ex-husband is hardly the same thing as taking home a stranger. There's a difference between self-control and self-denial."

She pulled her legs up against her body and turned her head, resting her cheek on her knees. It gave her a strange, sideways view of his concerned expression. She appreciated that he was at least trying to understand her perspective rather than fuming at her for leading him on, not that Nick ever would.

He'd always been a gentleman...just, a gentleman who ended up getting her naked more often than not.

"You may have a point," she conceded. After all, it wasn't so impromptu, her being attracted to him. She'd felt that pull most of her life. "I didn't realize the chemistry between us would still be so potent." In a smaller voice, she confessed, "It rattled me."

He held one hand out in front of him; they could both see his fingers trembled slightly. "I'm not exactly steady myself. I want you."

"I want you, too. But not like this." Sweaty and sore on a secondhand couch with bits of plaster and paint stuck in her hair? She'd been intentionally abstinent since joining the program. If she slept with him, it would be the first time she'd had sober sex in years, and she wanted to remember it as more than a savage haze. To savor it. To know that she was doing something deliberate and not just losing herself in a different kind of intoxication. "Go home, cool down. And after you've had a chance to think about it, ask me out. If you still want to."

"So you're not saying no?" he asked, looking cheerful again. "I just have to put some thought and effort into it?"

She chuckled. "That's not exactly how I meant it, but okay."

"You're worth the effort. I used to love that, planning how to get you alone, what I would say, where I wanted to touch you first. It'll be just like old times."

"No." She winced. They weren't seventeen anymore. "It won't be."

"All right." Nick leaned down, pressing a kiss to the top of her head. "It'll be like new times, then. Even better."

Chapter Thirteen

"Someone's in a good mood," Dawn commented with a raised eyebrow.

Pam looked up blankly from the pile of hair she was sweeping. "Why do you say that?" Had she been unconsciously beaming at the broom? She probably looked like an idiot.

"You were singing," Dawn said. "Again. Third different song today. You're better than the radio station—no commercials."

They'd had a busy Saturday morning, but were enjoying a brief lunchtime lull. Nancy had run out to make a deposit before the bank closed at one, and Beth was getting sandwiches for all of them. Dawn had just finished with a customer and didn't have another appointment for fifteen minutes.

"Huh. I didn't realize I was singing."

Dawn smirked. "So who is he?"

"A woman can sing without there being a man involved," Pam replied, stonewalling. She tried not to think about the way Nick had kissed her last night. "I sang professionally for years."

"Oh, come on," Dawn pleaded. "I tell you all the romantic details about me and Jer."

"Whether I want them or not," Pam grumbled good-naturedly.

Dawn put her hands on her ample hips. "Are you really not going to tell me?"

"I'm not sure there's anything to tell yet. Let's just say that, for the first time in a long time, there's a poss—"

The door to the beauty shop opened and both women turned automatically. It wasn't the woman with the next appointment, however. It was a young guy with skinny legs beneath his khaki shorts. His top half was mostly obscured by the large flower arrangement he carried.

"One of you Pam Wilson?" he asked from around the blooms.

"That would be her," Dawn said with a cat-who-ate-the-canary smile.

Oh. Pam's face warmed; she could feel the rosy blush creeping up her cheeks. *Nick, you shouldn't have.*

He apparently felt otherwise. The card read: Being with you is worth every effort, worth any wait. I'll be in touch soon.

Instead of signing it, he'd simply drawn that elongated, not-quite-closed heart shape she recognized from school. Passing notes had been forbidden in class, and teachers were known to be merciless to those caught—often reading the private messages aloud. So she and Nick had never used names anywhere on their letters; instead his signature had always been this same heart. It was such a small thing to have tears pricking the backs of her eyes, but she was moved that he remembered and would think to do it now.

She slipped the card into her pocket. "Is it all right if I put these on the front desk for everyone to enjoy?"

"Well, there is a strict salon policy that says you can only display personal gifts and bouquets if you tell your coworkers who they're from," Dawn deadpanned.

Pam nibbled at her lower lip. Dawn was a dear, longtime friend—who better to confide in? But for the first time in her life, Pam was afraid of being in the spotlight, superstitious that if she invited outside speculation, things might fall apart before they'd even begun.

"Oooh, flowers." Nancy strolled into the salon, her interest piqued. "I don't suppose they're for me? Clive and I had a bit of a spat, and it would be just like him to apologize this way."

"Sorry, they're Pam's," Dawn said with exaggerated sweetness. It was unlike her to be vindictive, but she'd made it clear on several occasions that she didn't approve of the way Nancy treated Pam.

"Oh," Nancy said flatly. She rolled her eyes. "You and Nick haven't changed since high school, always so eager to flaunt your relationship in front of everyone else." With that, she stomped toward the ladies' room at the back of the salon.

"She's crazy," Dawn pronounced. "That was years ago. You and Nick aren't... *Are* you?"

"I'm not sure," Pam said. Although the flowers seemed like a pretty positive indication.

"When did this happen?"

"I'm not sure about that either." Sometime between when he'd first shown up at Trudy's to let

Pam know she wasn't welcome in Mimosa and when he'd entreated her to meet their daughter, between his calling her after that meeting to make sure she wasn't tempted to drink and his making her lunch.

To say nothing of the wicked things he'd done to her on her couch.

"So what does this mean? Are the two of you back together?"

With a sigh, Pam carried the broom and dustpan into the storage closet. "Dawn, you can keep asking questions, but they won't do you much good. You'll notice 'I'm not sure' is the running theme here."

"Hmm." Dawn glanced toward the front door, which Pam didn't have a clear view of from inside the closet. "Do you think his family might have some idea of whether you're dating?"

"What do you mean, his family?" Oh, Lord. *His mother decided she couldn't afford a hit man and is coming to do me in herself.* It was more likely Faith who was visiting, although Pam would be disappointed in the girl if she disobeyed her dad again.

Pam poked her head out of the closet just in time to see Leigh Shepard—Pam couldn't recall her married name—enter the salon. The woman was carrying a basket on her arm as if she were stopping by on her way to Grandma's house.

"Afternoon, Dawn." Leigh flashed the woman a genuine smile. "Got time to squeeze me in today? Thought I'd get a trim and drop these cookies off for Pamela Jo." She glanced past Dawn, and the smile wobbled slightly when she spotted her former sister-in-law. "They're sort of a housewarming gift, I guess. I understand you had furniture moved out to Mae's old place this week."

"Thank you." Pam was touched. And deeply suspicious. Maybe she should have a lab in one of the bigger cities test the cookies before she ate any.

"Come on back," Dawn invited Leigh. "You want a shampoo first or are we doing a dry cut?"

As Leigh explained what she was in the mood for today, Nancy returned to the front of the salon, belting her smock over her black jeans and black turtleneck sweater. "What smells so good up here?" she asked no one in particular. "Beth back with the food already?"

"Actually," Pam replied, "Leigh brought me homemade cookies."

Nancy's lips compressed into a thin line that

ruined the effect of her pout-plumping gloss. "What, is it your birthday or something?"

Pam studied the bright bouquet and aromatic basket of chocolate cookies and grinned from ear to ear. "Or something."

"Did I catch you hard at work?"

Even though Pam knew the caller was going to be Nick before she answered—the number had flashed on the cell's display screen—hearing his voice still sent a thrill through her. "Not exactly." She'd actually been in the middle of a break, sitting out on the front step, listening to the cacophony of crickets and frogs and night birds now that dark had fallen. The sun was setting earlier and earlier each day, a clear mark that summer was behind them.

It's pretty out here. The thought shouldn't have surprised her; after all, she'd grown up with this same night music, the same stars twinkling overhead. She supposed "serene" just wasn't how she remembered her childhood home. Twenty minutes ago, she'd come out here with a glass of cold milk and a small plate stacked with cookies; now she was too relaxed to move. "I finally got around to eating those cookies Leigh gave me."

He chuckled. "Did you feed them to the ladies at the salon first and deem them safe after a forty-eight-hour period passed with no one's stomach needing to be pumped?"

"Nah, but that would have been so much better than my plan. I ignored the cookies for two days, then got the munchies and scarfed down four of them in one sitting. They're excellent."

"Her peacemaking cookies," he said affectionately. "Whenever she used to do something really mean to me, I'd get my very own batch a couple of days later."

"Not the worst policy I've ever heard." Forgiveness wasn't always an easy concept; cookies could help.

"Speaking of Leigh, she's actually the reason I'm calling," he said.

"Oh?" Pam tried not to sound miffed. He wasn't calling, perhaps, to tell her about an interesting movie coming to theaters or to let her know about a restaurant that had opened in Mimosa during her years away? It had been nearly a week since Pam had advised him to ask her out, but so far, nothing. They'd had a couple of good conversations in the four days since he'd kissed her. But on the possibility of going out, he'd said nothing.

Zip, bupkus, nada, squat.

"Leigh has sons," he said, sounding extremely cheerful about this piece of trivia. "So occasionally she likes to do female bonding stuff with Faith. And next Monday just so happens to be a teacher in-service day at the middle school, giving the students a three-day weekend. Leigh has offered to take Faith out of town to do some outlet shopping and a riverboat luncheon cruise. Looks like I'll have the house all to myself for a couple of days."

"You don't say?" Pam's heart was so light it was floating in her chest. "You know, I've always liked your sister."

He laughed. "But not as much as you like me, right? I'm the one who sent you flowers."

"Which I already called and thanked you for," she drawled, mock-bored even while she was grinning like crazy. "That's old news."

"Oh, I see." He played along. "You're of the 'what have you done for me lately?' mind-set. Tough lady to impress."

Yeah, right. All he had to do was smile at her and she melted inside. "Exactly."

"Do I get any credit for nudging Leigh in the long-weekend direction?" he asked. "I may have let it slip that I was hoping Faith would find ways to occupy her time this weekend that didn't include hanging around with Morgan."

"So you're saying you secretly masterminded the whole trip? Sneaky," she said approvingly.

"You haven't heard my ace up the sleeve yet. I cook! Want to come check it out for yourself on Saturday? My place, say, seven o'clock?"

She managed not to squeal her acceptance like some girl Faith's age being asked to sit at lunch with the cutest guy in school. "Sounds perfect."

As they ended their phone call, Pam rocketed to her feet, brimming with renewed energy. The hours between now and Saturday would drag, and she was determined to keep them as full as possible.

It did not bode well for one's romantic evening, Pam decided, when merely the act of lifting your sore arm to knock on the front door made you cringe. *Mental note: doorbell, next time.* She'd just be sure to ring with a finger she *hadn't* squashed with a hammer yesterday. Her entire upper body felt like one big bruise.

Nick answered the door quickly as if he'd been hovering on the other side, anxious for her arrival. "Right on time," he praised. His gaze slid down her red jersey dress, a simple scoop neck with a far more daring scooped back. "And you look amazing."

"Thank you." *And thank you, Dawn.* Her friend had come over to the house today, not only to offer her services in the wallpapering department, but also to help with Pam's hair and makeup.

"Please come in," he said. "We have about twenty minutes until dinner's ready. Can I pour you a glass of w—oh, crap. I'm so sorry."

She was able to laugh it off. "Don't be. It's not the first time someone's asked me that question. I'll stick with sweet tea or, if you don't have any, filtered water. But you should feel free to have wine or anything else you'd like to drink tonight."

"I'm fine with water, too," he said promptly. "The sight of you in that red dress is all the buzz I need for one evening."

She stretched up on her toes to press a quick kiss to his cheek. "Flatterer. So what's on the menu for tonight?"

He rocked back, giving her a wolfish smile. "Well…"

Pam smacked him lightly on his arm. "The culinary menu, Mr. One Track Mind!"

"Shrimp pomodoro over angel-hair pasta with Caesar salad. I made the dressing myself. And dessert is a surprise, but trust me, it's not store bought."

"You showing off for me?" She liked it.

"Just demonstrating that I think you're worth the effort. Now if you'll excuse me, I have to stir the sauce."

She followed him into the kitchen, where she kicked off her shoes. It was a shame, really—they were very sexy shoes—but it was just so homey and inviting in here. She wanted to be comfortable, enjoy the delicious smells and Nick's company.

They talked nonstop while he finished preparing their dinner. He told her about how he'd earned Donald Bauer's respect when he was only twenty, juggling a construction job and parenthood. Bauer Construction had been started by Donald's father, but the man had no sons who could take it over after him. When Nick returned to Mimosa from North Carolina, Donald had not just rehired him, he'd started grooming him to manage the entire organization.

They discussed Pam's renovations on the house, which were going really well. While Aunt Julia couldn't do any jobs that required heavy lifting, she had an eye for color and detail and had become Pam's unofficial decorating consultant. Pam also mentioned that several of the people she'd met at the local AA meetings had stopped by, seeming to find the manual labor as cathartic as she did; respecting the confidentiality of other members, she didn't tell Nick that one of those people worked for him.

"Voilà!" Nick stepped back from two perfectly plated meals, spreading his hands in front of him. He winked at her. "Damn, I'm good."

"I believe that's for me to decide," she teased.

He came around the other side of the counter to sit with her. "My daughter would be so jealous. This is one of her favorite dishes."

Pam bit her lip. "She doesn't know, does she? That I'm here?"

He shook his head. "I thought it best not to tell her. It's not like I consider you some shameful secret. I just…"

"You did the right thing." This could be confusing for a girl. Heck, it was confusing for Pam.

It's not rocket science. He's a very attractive man you care a lot about, and you're two consenting adults enjoying a romantic evening. Beyond that… Well, she wasn't sure, but the policy of taking one day at a time had been serving her well so far.

They talked more about Faith and the foods she liked. "It's hard for me to believe that the young woman who now requests chicken alfredo or shrimp pomodoro as her birthday dinner is the same one who used to consider hot dogs sliced up in macaroni the most sought-after meal in the world," Nick said fondly.

Pam grinned. "What's not to believe—they're practically all three the same dishes. Protein, pasta, a little sauce."

"Yeah. I'm sure fine Italian restaurants will start serving mac and weenies any day now."

They also discussed Pam's aunt and uncle. She talked about how amazing it was to almost feel as if she had functional parents for the first time in her life. But she stopped short of confiding that they'd once entertained the idea of challenging Mae for custody. That seemed too heavy a topic for the fun, flirty meal they were sharing.

"That was wonderful," Pam said, rolling her shoulders. If her neck and arms didn't ache, the last hour and a half would have qualified as heavenly.

Nick tilted his head. "Glad you enjoyed the

food, but do you realize you keep rubbing your neck and grimacing?"

"Have I?" she asked sheepishly. *Nuts.* What was the point of Dawn making her look beautiful if Pam was going to ruin it by making contorted faces all night? "I took some ibuprofen before I came over, but I guess it hasn't really kicked in."

"Did you hurt yourself?" Even as he asked, he was scanning her, presumably for wounds, although she didn't think her sore muscles were visible.

"Don't laugh, but I was excited about tonight—"

"You weren't the only one," he assured her.

"And I was trying to keep myself really busy. You know, to make it get here faster, like going to sleep early on Christmas Eve. I may have overdone it." Her efforts had paid off at the house, which was starting to really resemble something people would pay money to live in, but she hadn't exactly kept her body in top physical shape over the past decade.

Nick brightened. "I think I can help."

"I don't think I can take another ibuprofen yet."

"No, what I had in mind is way better than painkillers. You trust me, right?"

More than anyone I've ever known. "Sure."

He had hopped off the stool and was carrying their plates to the sink. "What you need is a trip to the Shepard Spa."

"Sounds promising. You guys have a hot tub I don't know about?"

"Nope. I just need a few minutes to get things set up." He took her by the hand. "Here, you come with me." They went in to a small den, which had a much smaller television set than the main living room. He pointed the remote at it. "Can you find something to watch?"

"I guess." As if she were going to concentrate on a few minutes of TV? She'd be too curious about what he was doing.

"Ten minutes, max," he promised. "You stay put." Then he shut the door and was gone.

Pam wiggled her bare toes in happy anticipation.

He opened the door again a few minutes later. "All set."

They returned to the living room, and Pam saw that he'd been busy. The only illumination in the room was assorted candles burning on the fireplace mantel and the coffee table. Instrumental music played softly in the background. And he'd scooted back some of the smaller pieces of furniture to make a clearing in the floor. A pallet of sheets and blankets awaited, with one pristine white bedsheet still neatly folded on top.

"You've had massages before, right?" Nick asked. "I'll just duck out of the room while you undress, only as far as you're comfortable, cover up with the sheet and let me know when you're ready."

She turned to him with a smirk. "I'll give you this, Nicholas Shepard, your ploys to get me out of my clothes have gotten classier."

"You ain't seen nothing yet. It gets better," he promised. "I just have to go in the kitchen for one final thing. Call me when you're ready."

"Okay." Watching him walk away, she experienced one small moment of shyness. This man had known every inch of her body when she was in peak physical condition.

Then again, he'd seen firsthand what she'd looked like pregnant and that hadn't dimmed his ardor for her. She slipped her dress over her head then paused, considering. Should she leave on the rest? Just remove her bra?

Deciding to go for it, she quickly peeled off all of her clothes before she could change her mind, folding the lacy undergarments inside her dress. Then she laid down on her stomach and stretched the extra sheet over her. "Okay!" *Ready as I'll ever be.*

When Nick came back, he was barefoot and had removed his button-down shirt, leaving him in pants and a white T-shirt. "I don't have any body oil," he said as he sat next to her, "but I think you'll like this."

He held his hand several inches above her back, and something cool and feathery hit her skin.

"What is that?" she murmured. It felt like powdered silk as he began to trace it over her in light circles.

"Corn starch."

She'd never realized how soft it was. "Mmm. Nice."

She closed her eyes. There was a perfect balance between the strength in Nick's strong hands and the gentleness of his touch as he ran his fingers over her skin. He gradually applied more and more pressure until her knotted muscles were pliant and warm.

He also, very gradually, started to make larger circles as he traveled up and down her back, dipping below the base of her spine, toward the curve of her butt, then making his way back up, kneading his thumbs and the heels of his palms against her. When he reached the tops of her shoulders, he let his hands skim down over her sides, toward her chest. But just when she thought he would take it further, that the body-melting massage would morph into something else, he'd start the slow journey to the center of her back again.

She felt incredible—pampered, lavished— but her body was also starting to hum with anticipation, wanting more. He bent down to kiss her on the back of the neck, and she made a low, approving noise.

"Thank you for letting me do this," he murmured, as if the massage had somehow been as good for him as it had for her. "I could touch you all night."

She lifted up on one elbow to smile at him. "There's an idea." Then she rolled the rest of the way over, letting the sheet fall where it may without modesty.

Nick froze, seemingly not even breathing as he drank in the sight of her. She gave him a moment, then reached for him, pulling him down to kiss her.

"You have wonderful hands," she whispered. Grinning against his lips, she trailed her own hand down over his erection. "You have wonderful everything."

"I don't want to rush you," he teased as she tugged his shirt over his head. "Maybe we should slow down. I'm not sure we've thought about this long enough."

She shoved at his shoulder, and he obligingly fell to his back.

"I've been thinking about this all week," she said, dotting kisses over his chest while her hand strayed lower. "That's probably long enough."

He smiled up at her. "Then you're not worried about losing control anymore?"

"Actually—" she lifted his hand, pressed a kiss to his palm, and then placed it on her breast "—I was kind of hoping we both would."

He was in clear agreement, but no discernible hurry. He let her finish undressing him, groaning as she frequently stopped along the way to relearn his body. There was a deceptively languorous quality to their caresses that didn't quite match the avid, alert way he watched her or the throb of arousal building inside her. She straddled him, leaning down so that he could suckle her. But before long, they shifted position, their motions fluid and intuitively synchronized.

She planned to be back on top later, but for now, it was bliss to have him over her, poised to enter her. She was slick and ready for him but still fluttery with nerves—it had been a long time since she'd done this. It had been a lifetime since she'd done it with the right man.

He slid into her in one smooth thrust that stole her breath. It didn't hurt, but it definitely took a moment of adjustment for her out-of-practice body. Then pleasure and instinct took over, her body rising and falling to meet his. Somewhere in the middle of it, they did roll over again, and she found herself controlling the tempo, squeezing her muscles around him, not a sore spot on her entire body. She felt *so* good, gloriously alive and exhilarated and free.

Nick reached between their bodies, stroking his thumb over her and heightening the climax that had already begun to spiral through her. She called out his name, heard him answer with a wordless shout as he drove into her. He clasped her to him in a fierce hug, their combined ragged breathing drowning out the music that had been playing earlier. Or maybe the CD had simply stopped.

"Wow." She blew out a breath, puffing her damp bangs away from her face. It was a lot hotter in Nick's house than it had been when she first arrived. "Best date ever."

He nuzzled her neck. "Doesn't have to be

over yet. We have the house to ourselves until tomorrow night."

Tomorrow. Their time together would pass too quickly, but for now, she planned to make the most of it.

Chapter Fourteen

"You know how last week I pointed out that you were singing all the time without even realizing it?" Dawn asked. "This morning you've been singing *and* dancing."

"Well, why shouldn't I be happy?" Pam asked, wiggling in a little side-to-side shake. "It's a beautiful September day, the house renovations have far exceeded my expectations, I get to work with all of you wonderful women— you're particularly lovely today, Nancy!"

The woman shot Pam an unamused look but refrained, probably due to their customers, from shooting the finger. Then Nancy's scowl deepened. "Oh, spare me. Here comes lover boy."

Dawn grinned, nudging Pam in the elbow with her ribs. "Guess you two can't get enough of each other, huh?"

The ladies met Nick with innocent we-weren't-all-just-talking-about-you smiles when he came through the door.

He walked up to the reception desk, where Pam was doing computer work, and Dawn flitted off to "see if that load of laundry is dry yet."

"Welcome to C-3," Pam chirped.

He grinned at her. "I'd like to make an appointment. Preferably with you, for lunch."

She laughed. "Your daughter would have a fit if she knew you were here. Didn't you give her some speech about not stalking me while I was at work?"

"Aren't you familiar with the expression 'Do as I say, not as I do'?"

"Is that the fancy version of 'Because I said so'? Lunch sounds good in theory," she said, glancing at the open spreadsheet on the computer screen, "but I don't think today's going to work. I'm right in the middle of something I need to finish. Besides, I leave today at two and wasn't really planning on a lunch break. Aunt Julia has a project she needs my help on."

Julia had been lamenting that while her jewelry-making had taken off better than expected, her clientele was mostly women of a certain age. She was trying to vary her style enough to attract a younger market.

"I sit in my vendor stall at community festivals and watch these teenagers run around," she'd mused. *"And it got me to thinking—some of them have a bigger budget for mad money than their mothers! Allowances, babysitting funds and no monthly bills."*

Pam had come up with a few ideas for a funkier "line" of jewelry, including earrings made from guitar picks.

Which reminded her. "Have you and Faith ever revisited the guitar discussion?" she asked Nick.

"A little," he said. "If she's serious about it, I may get her a guitar for Christmas. She wants to learn enough about sheet music that she can do notations for some of the songs she's written."

Pam took a deep breath. "Well, I'm not offering lessons—I'm too rusty for one thing, and it takes more than just talent to be able to teach someone else how to develop that talent. But how would you feel about letting me borrow Faith for a couple of afternoons? She's in the right demographic to give Julia and me her opinion on jewelry designs. In return for her

help, I'll show her some basics on the guitar.
The house is finally in good enough shape that
she wouldn't require a hard hat and an emergency contact card."

"Sounds like a win-win for everyone," he
said. "I think she'd love that. In fact, maybe
I'll swing by the school and have lunch with
her. As long as I don't try to be funny in front
of her friends, she seems to like seeing me periodically."

"So you'll talk to her about my idea?" Pam
knew it would mean a lot to Julia to meet her
great-niece, even if it were only under the guise
of getting a twelve-year-old's perspective.

"I'll ask her, but I guarantee the answer
is going to be an enthusiastic yes. The only
real question is, how soon do you want to get
started?"

Even from the sidewalk out in front of the little house, Nick could hear the feminine laughter
inside. Pam's uninhibited laugh, Faith's slightly
higher giggle, making her sound like the ador-
able little girl she'd been not so long ago, and
was that even a restrained chuckle from Julia?
They sounded as if they were having so much
fun that he almost hated to knock on the door.

As it turned out, he had to knock repeatedly

before they finally heard him. Pam opened the door, her eyes bright and cheeks flushed with humor.

"Come on in."

He would, but he was temporarily too dumbstruck to move. "You did all this?" he asked, staring past her.

She followed his gaze, taking in the finished living room walls, the gleaming new light fixture overhead and the recently hung shelf—on top of which sat a framed picture of Ed and Julia, a small flowering plant and a radio. "Not by myself. I told you, I've had help."

She ticked off names on her fingers. "Uncle Ed stopped by whenever he could, sometimes bringing a guy or two from the warehouse. Aunt Julia showed up one day with two volunteers from her sewing circle. Beth and Dawn have both been out here to pitch in at various times, and some of the people at AA meetings who are newly sober and still restless have discovered that showing up here around ten o'clock at night gives them something constructive to do and keeps them out of bars."

Nick frowned over the idea of her opening the door to people she didn't know well after ten o'clock, but admitted, "The place has never looked better."

"I'll give you the complete tour when it's done." She ushered him inside.

"Hey, Dad." Faith and Julia appeared at the edge of the living room. His daughter was smiling yet looked disappointed at the same time. "Do we have to leave already? Pam never even pulled out the guitar!"

"Sorry about that," Pam said as she smoothed the girl's hair. "Next time, I promise. You can come back tomorrow if it's all right with your father. I guess we just got too caught up with everything else."

"Evening, Julia." Nick smiled at Pam's aunt, glad that the two women had finally formed a strong family bond. Pam deserved to have that in her life. He never lost sight of the fact that he'd been blessed in that respect, even on days when his mother or sister exasperated the hell out of him.

Julia inclined her head. "Nick, always nice to see you. Thanks for letting us borrow your beautiful daughter for the afternoon. She's been quite a help."

Faith lifted her chin, adopting a self-important expression. "I'm in jewelry design now. Maybe someday I'll have my own accessory line."

He arched an eyebrow. "What happened to NASA?"

"Oh, Father." She rolled her eyes. "I plan to do both. Duh."

Pam tried to smother a laugh, and he glanced toward her, meeting her gaze, recognizing the same pride in her expression that welled within him. *Our daughter, the jewelry-designing aeronautics engineer.* He was the luckiest damn man alive.

Faith scooped up her backpack from where it sat on the floor next to the couch. "So I'll see you both again tomorrow?"

"It will have to be later because I work until five tomorrow," Pam said, "but it's okay with me if it's okay with your dad. You have to get your homework done first, though."

"Deal!" She spun around, pinning Nick with wide, beseeching eyes. "It's okay with you, right, Dad?"

"Sure. You guys seemed like you were having a good time."

Faith's eyes twinkled, a merry gold today. "Pam was telling us about this one time when you were fourteen and wanted to go to the mall and get your ear pierced because you thought it would make you cool, but Grandma Gwendolyn said absolutely not, and you asked Pam to try to pierce it for you."

Nick groaned. "Pamela Jo! You're supposed

to tell her only the stories about how well I listened to my parents and how dedicated I was to my academic career."

Pam grinned at him. "I see. I'll try to come up with one of those stories for next time. But off the top of my head, I can't seem to recall…"

"Come along, Faith," he said with mock severity. "We have to be going now."

His daughter whistled Beethoven all the way to the car, which made him think that Aunt Julia had been the one who got to pick the background music for their jewelry-making session.

"So, good afternoon?" Nick asked as they both got buckled.

"Stupendous day! You will not even believe what happened at school after you visited me, Daddy." His daughter was positively vibrating with giddy excitement. "Right after you left!"

Nick had been relieved that she'd been pleased by his unannounced presence at lunch. He thought that even her world-weary friend Morgan had looked a bit wistful. Maybe Morgan wasn't such a rotten kid; her family had been ripped apart by an ugly divorce, which probably amplified her attitude.

"What happened?" he asked dutifully.

"He asked me! Bryce actually asked me!"

"Should I know this Bryce?" Nick hoped he

didn't sound as panicked as he felt. *Bryce who? Asked her what? I'll kill him.* Apparently all fathers possessed a dormant homicidal gene that didn't make itself known until some boy asked their daughter for something. *Please, God, let it have been to borrow her pencil.*

"Bryce Watkins. I've liked him ever since he was my lab partner when we had to dissect earthworms."

Ah, young love.

"And he asked me to the autumn social! He actually asked me."

"That's wonderful, honey. You seem pretty jazzed up about this."

"Yeah, you have no idea how hard it was not to spill the beans this afternoon! I wanted to tell Pam," she said. "But I wanted to tell you first."

Nick's throat tightened at the gesture. He knew it must have required monumental effort for a twelve-year-old girl not to share the news of a big crush asking her on a date. *Date?* The enormity of the event hit him. Her first date. He had a sharp pain in his abdomen that probably signaled an ulcer.

"I can't wait to tell Pam," Faith enthused. "You think she can help me pick out a dress? No offense, but I bet she's better at it than you."

"None taken. You can ask her about it when you see her tomorrow."

Faith babbled happily for the rest of the ride home, and Nick did his best to follow her patter, but his mind was on autopilot. He found himself thinking about Pam. His daughter wasn't the only one with a big crush.

Crush, hell. I'm in love with her.

He doubted now that he'd ever truly stopped loving her, not completely. He'd been very angry with her for a very long time, interspersed with periods where he'd managed to shove his feelings down and not think about her. It was like he'd had emotional frostbite. When it came to his romantic relationships, he'd had a certain unshakable numbness. Seeing her again had thawed him out in a way that wasn't always pleasant. He'd had more temperamental outbursts in Pam's first two weeks back in Mimosa than during his entire marriage to Jenna.

But there was no escaping the truth—he wanted the same thing now that he'd wanted at sixteen, to have a family and a forever with Pamela Jo Wilson. Was it his imagination, or did Faith want that, too? She could have suggested a shopping trip with her aunt Leigh or even Morgan and her mother, but she wanted to spend that with Pam instead.

Shockingly, he thought that Pam would actually agree to go dress shopping. She'd probably even be cheerful about the prospect, which made her a completely different woman than the one who'd backed away from him a month ago with panic-stricken eyes when he'd asked her to have a milk shake with her daughter. She'd changed during her time in Mimosa. As far as he could tell, all for the better.

The big question was, had she changed her mind about staying?

Her aunt left after dinner, and now Pam was all alone in the house again. Normally around this time, she would sit outside for a few minutes and listen to night fall around her. It had become something of a meditative ritual. However, rain had started sprinkling shortly after Nick and Faith left and it was now pouring.

Pam found herself drifting from one room to the next, compiling a mental checklist. The plumber was due on Friday; the fresh coat of paint on the bedroom walls looked great, but she had to hang all of the new trim around doors and floor; she'd received a call that her order of glass was in and would be delivered tomorrow—several window panes had to be replaced. Granted, the external landscaping was…well, nonexistent, and the hole in the kitchen where a dishwasher should be bothered her, but the house was becoming downright cozy. It had meant a lot to have Faith here today and feel proud of the work she'd done, not ashamed that this house was her past.

Recalling her promise to Faith, Pam dragged her feet to the closet where she'd stored the guitar case as soon as she'd taken up residence. Pam withdrew the case, which was heavier than she remembered, and carried it to the couch. Inside was the guitar that had represented so many of her dreams, almost none of which had materialized. At one time, she'd looked at this guitar and seen her entire future. Now it was the wood and string embodiment of a million mistakes.

Just looking at it made her thirsty.

It's a guitar. No more, no less. She'd faced down an enraged mother on more than one occasion, often wondering if this would be the time Mae actually lost it enough to wallop her. She'd faced her own addiction and hadn't let changing locations become an excuse for dropping the program. Surely she could face a single acoustic guitar.

Play it again, Pam.

Lips twitching in a sardonic smile, she

strummed a couple of notes from "As Time Goes By," but it wasn't a song she knew well. The guitar deserved better. After a moment, she started "Amazing Grace," stopped, then started again, singing along this time. She progressed to faster country songs and classic rock, attempting some Skynyrd and Boston numbers, frustrated at how much she got wrong. It felt like she was trying to play with someone else's fingers.

The thought stopped her, and she quit in the middle of a Rolling Stones song. Someone else. How much of her was the same Pamela Jo Wilson who'd grown up in this house, hating her mother and loving guitar, and how much was simply Pam—a slightly older, slightly wiser, more tired, more realistic, much more centered person?

Recalling her wild weekend with Nick, spent mostly on his living room floor and tangled in his bed, she grinned. *Maybe not so old or tired.*

She settled into Clapton's "Wonderful Tonight," which had been the theme for her and Nick's senior prom and kept right on playing for hours, taking only the occasional break, until her voice started to go and she'd developed blisters. When she accidentally sliced one of those blisters open, she put the guitar aside, blinking in surprise. It was morning?

Hazy sunlight was starting to filter through the windows. The rain had stopped, and the night was over.

For two afternoons in a row, Pam and Faith worked on basic chords. The second afternoon, Faith asked if she could sing one of her original compositions, but she lost her nerve at the last minute.

"Don't worry about it," Pam said. "Maybe next time. Tell you what, I have to go hammer some decorative molding back into place. You want to practice by yourself for a little while?"

"That would be great." Faith looked a bit relieved to have time alone to go over what she'd learned. It was difficult to improve when you didn't have your own guitar to practice on; Pam wondered if Nick would be able to hold out until Christmas.

Faith had thought the building-up-calluses part sounded gross, but other than that, she seemed like a natural.

On Sunday, Pam and Faith decided to forego music lessons in favor of dress shopping. Pam had hoped to get a head start on it the day before—with the big dance coming the following Saturday, they were cutting it close—but the salon had been packed from open to closing.

Dawn hadn't been kidding about all the alumni in town getting ready for various events this week. Nick, as a former Mimosa High football star, was planning to take Faith to the big game Friday night and they'd asked Pam to join them.

While Pam drove her daughter to the closest mall, about twenty minutes out of town, Faith implored her to talk to Nick.

"He's making me nuts kidding around about signing up to chaperone the dance," Faith said. "At least I hope he's kidding. That's the problem. He might be serious! You have to do something. Keep him busy that night."

"Excuse me?"

"Take him bowling, see a movie. Whatever people your age do," Faith said.

"People *my* age?" Pam pulled a face. "Word of advice, kid. If you're trying to get a woman to do you a favor, don't make her feel like she's older than dirt."

"Oh, I didn't mean that. You guys are both way younger than most of my friends' parents. I just meant, Dad's never really dated very much, so I'm not sure what exactly he'd do on one."

If Nick hadn't dated, it had to have been his choice. He was a gorgeous, successful guy with broad shoulders to lean on and a wicked sense of humor. Or had his dating been curtailed because of Faith? Maybe he'd worried how she would handle the idea or he'd simply been too busy as a single parent. Or were women resistant to the idea of being with a man who came with a ready-made family?

Pam felt herself getting indignant on his behalf. Any woman would be lucky to have Nick and Faith! They… She stopped, wincing at the irony and trying not to lose her breath at the realization of all she'd sacrificed. Today was her first mother-daughter outing with Faith. If Pam hadn't run twelve years ago, she would have driven her to school and dentist appointments and maybe music lessons. It was a sure bet that, hearing her daughter's voice, she would have encouraged her to develop that talent.

The thought gave her pause…because she actually believed it. She'd left because she hadn't loved her own child, but whatever the past had held, Pam knew she could love her now. It was far easier to imagine herself cheering her daughter on than it was to picture herself belittling her or lashing out at her.

"How old were you when I was born?" Faith asked suddenly.

"Uh… How about we listen to some music?" Pam didn't know how to handle the topic of her and Nick's romantic history. On the one hand, she was tempted to use her teen pregnancy as a teachable moment, demonstrating why the only real way to be careful was to wait. Then again, she didn't want to make it sound like anyone regretted Faith's existence.

"All right." Faith shot her a knowing look, but turned on the radio. Before long, they were singing together, naturally harmonizing. Pam actually stopped at one point, just to enjoy the way her daughter was belting out the lyrics.

She's better than I was. Unpolished, sure, but gifted. But Faith hadn't let that single gift define her. She was a well-rounded girl with varied interests and countless possibilities for the future. Again, Pam thought to herself what a good job Nick had done as a parent. Of course, he'd told her how much Leigh and his mother had helped over the years. *Crap. Next time I see Gwendolyn, I'm going to have to be nice to her.*

At the first store, Pam steered Faith away from a rack of dresses that, while technically the right size, were completely inappropriate for her age. "Not those."

Faith laughed. "I know. Dad's head would explode. Morgan has this insanely convoluted plan for how to get the dress she really wants to wear—which her mom won't let her—into her locker at school so that she can slip away from the gymnasium during the dance and change. Tasha and I keep telling her it won't work. The side hallways are locked during special events so no one can sneak off and get in trouble."

Pam paused, wondering how much she could safely interfere without alienating Faith. "You and Morgan are pretty good friends?"

Faith nodded promptly. "She was the first person who was nice to me when Dad and I moved here. And she totally knows what it's like to deal with divorce, not that my problems were as bad as hers. I was never that close to Jenna. Plus, even during the divorce, Jenna and Dad didn't scream at each other. You should hear Morgan's parents."

Pam winced, feeling unwanted sympathy for the Bad Seed. "My mom screamed all the time when I was a kid. That can be rough."

"Who was your best friend?" Faith wanted to know. "Ms. Lewin?"

Much as Pam liked Dawn, then and now, Pam had never wanted to burden her with the realities of life at the Wilson house. Dawn had spent the night only once, and had watched with wide-eyed shock as Mae staggered drunkenly down the hallway with the cordless phone, arguing loudly with some guy she'd been seeing.

"Actually," Pam said, "I'd have to say your

dad was my best friend. He's a great guy. Do me a favor? Listen to him. Sometimes it will seem like more fun, or at least cooler, to do what Morgan or someone else tells you to do. But if your father tells you it's a bad idea or your heart tells you it's a bad idea, walk away. Especially if alcohol is involved."

Faith regarded her seriously. "Is that why you used to drink too much, because some friends talked you into it?"

"I drank for a lot of reasons, none of them good. You're genetically predisposed, so you may need to be even more careful than your friends. And one or two really hateful jerks might even tease you, but that's preferable to stumbling and breaking your arm. Or wrapping your car around a tree. Got it?"

Faith nodded. "Got it."

"All right, enough with the after school special. Let's find you a killer dress."

Mimosa was abuzz with special events related to the homecoming. As far as Pam could tell, the week was crazy busy for everyone. Business at the salon never let up. Faith didn't have time to practice guitar chords because she was studying for the school year's first round of major exams. Nick's construction crews doubled productivity now that they were working in humane temperatures. And Julia took two private orders for jewelry. One was for Faith, who had insisted on paying for a great necklace to go with her dress for the dance. The other order was a bit more substantial—a woman getting ready to take a cruise with her five sisters had commissioned a set of jewelry for each sister, all of similar design but with slightly different colors and stones.

For the first half of the week, Pam enjoyed the whirl of people and activity, but by Friday, she was frazzled. She was in the salon's laundry room, adding detergent to a load and counting the hours until the end of her shift, when Beth called her to the front.

"Pam, you've got a delivery from a florist up here."

Had Nick sent her flowers again? She wracked her mind, trying to figure out what the occasion was. It was possible he just wanted to say thanks for her help with Faith's dress, but they'd brought that home days ago. He'd fussed over his daughter, who looked too much like "an elegant young woman—can't you go in pigtails and overalls instead?" But it was easy to tell he approved of their choice.

Curious, Pam quickly set the dials on the

washer and headed to the front desk. Once she saw the long box, she started laughing and couldn't stop. "Seriously?" she asked no one in particular. "He sent me a homecoming mum?"

It was tradition at the high school for guys to get their girlfriends one of these huge adornments. At the top, a fluffy white mum was centered in ribbons of blue and gold, the high school's colors. From there, long blue and gold ribbons trailed nearly to the floor, many with letters or decals on them. The sparkling foil letters on one of her ribbons spelled out Mimosa High; another read NS and PJW. Among the ribbons were chains of gold plastic microphones and guitars, as well as gold football helmets. It was incredibly gaudy.

Dawn stopped short when she saw it, wrinkling her nose uncertainly. "That is *something,* isn't it? I can't tell if he's crazy about you or trying to punish you."

Pam grinned at the eyesore. "What does it say about me that I kind of love it?"

"That you two are made for each other."

"You actually wore it." Nick stood at the front gate of the football stadium, grinning as she approached. Pam had ridden over with Dawn, but Nick had promised to get her home afterward. They would probably take Faith for a milk shake after the game.

"Of course I wore it! I'm just sorry I didn't have time to make a blue-and-gold arm garter for you." She'd entertained the idea for a few minutes even as she'd known she didn't have the time, materials or energy.

Frankly, she wasn't sure she had the energy for tonight. Part of her had wanted to simply curl up under a comforter and go to bed early. It wasn't just the hectic week, it was a groundless melancholy that had been growing all evening.

As she walked toward Nick, she had to kick ribbons free as they tried to tangle around her legs. "Fair warning—this thing trips me, I sue."

He laughed. "I believe you. I know how much you want to buy a dishwasher for that house."

"Not to mention roof repairs and a ton of stuff for the backyard."

On her skills and budget, though, she'd come about as far as she could. While she knew that roof repairs would come up during a property inspection, she thought it would be more a point of negotiation for closing costs, not enough to scare away prospective buyers. It wasn't a half-bad little house. The foundation was solid and the potential was there.

It was time to put it on the market.

"Faith's already inside," Nick said. "She and this Bryce kid are sitting a couple of rows in front of us. Enough room that we won't be eavesdropping on their conversation, but we should be able to see if he tries anything funny. Oh, and I hope you don't mind, but..."

"Yes?"

"We're sitting with Leigh and A.J."

At the mention of his sister, she sighed. "Joy. No, that's fine, I can get along with anybody for one night." Especially when she was too drained to be feisty. "I don't suppose she brought more cookies with her?"

"Sorry, no. If you're hungry, we can hit the concessions stand."

"I was kidding about the cookies, but a soft drink sounds pretty good." Maybe the caffeine would give her the jolt she needed to get pumped up for the game.

It seemed like the entire county had turned out for the football game, and she held Nick's hand to keep from losing him in the crowd. At one point, a man jostled into her with significant forward momentum. The force of impact separated her from Nick. She staggered slightly but didn't fall. Meanwhile, rather than stop in the middle of pedestrian traffic, Nick let himself get swept into the crowd. She saw him stop at the side of the walkway a few yards ahead, waiting for her.

"Sorry," the man said. He had a little girl on his shoulders and was walking with a woman who had an even younger toddler at her hip.

"I'm all right." Pam did a double take, recognizing him as Jake Stein from AA. She smiled, but he wasn't really focused on her. His eyes look glazed. "Jake, are you okay?"

He didn't bother answering. His only response was a puff of air blown through his lips, a not-quite raspberry that made it clear he was annoyed by her question.

"I'm sorry, you are...?" The woman next to him, who must have been Mrs. Stein, darted her gaze from Pam to Jake. "Honey, do you know this woman?"

He gave a shrug that bounced the little girl on his shoulders and made her giggle. "It's M'mosa. Everyone knows everyone. C'mon, let's get the girls to the bleachers. She's heavy."

Pam stood to the side of the narrow walkway as the family passed. Was it her imagination, or was Jake's gait unsteady? It was possibly the result of walking with a fifty-pound child on his shoulders, for all she knew. But her misgivings were strong enough that instead of turning toward Nick and getting those soft drinks, she stood planted where she was, unable to take her eyes away from the Stein family. When she'd been a kid, she'd developed a sense of impending doom that always started with the pit of her stomach.

You have an overactive imagination, and you were already in an irrationally bleak mood. She was advising herself to shake it off and get her soda when the man staggered again in the crowd. Pam's mind registered what was going to happen a split second before her eyes processed it.

Jake pitched forward with enough force that the little girl toppled from his shoulders and fell with a heart-rending cry to the pavement below.

Chapter Fifteen

Considering all the people jammed onto the walkway, Pam reached the Stein family pretty quickly. Jake's wife was trying to assess the shrieking girl's injuries while also juggling her shrieking younger sister, who was unharmed but startled. Jake wasn't even attempting to help. Instead he was sitting on the grass nearby, shaking his head and muttering to himself.

When Pam got close enough, she saw that he'd started to cry. She wanted to shake him—his wife had enough to deal with in two crying babies. Mrs. Stein shouldn't have to cope with her sobbing husband, who, unless Pam was wrong, had caused this accident in the first place.

"Oh, God." Pam was startled by the amount of blood. It hadn't been immediately obvious in the dark, but the wailing girl had turned her head in Pam's direction and one of the overhead lights caught her face. Her cherubic features, lit oddly bluish, were smeared with dark blood. Pam felt faint for a minute but pushed forward.

"Here," she offered to Mrs. Stein. "Would you like me to hold the little one?"

The girls' mother, clearly trying not to cry herself, nodded gratefully as she passed over the youngest of the two, freeing her up to examine the thrashing child more carefully. In an attempt to find the silver lining, Pam told herself that, given the rapid motion of the little girl's limbs, obviously she hadn't broken an arm or leg.

Pam patted the girl she held on the back, making shushing noises. She was distantly aware of the crowd parting around her as uniformed guards carrying first-aid kits reached the scene. The injured girl's shrill cries had subsided to a sort of hysterical snuffling, and Pam caught snatches of explanation from the guard. She'd knocked a tooth out on the concrete and apparently all face and head wounds bled terribly. They were advising Mrs. Stein to take her to the E.R. to check for a concussion and possibly for stitches.

During this conversation, Pam glanced over at where Jake sat. He had stopped talking to himself and was guzzling from a water bottle she hadn't seen before, probably retrieved from inside his jacket. The dark liquid he was belting back wasn't water.

You bastard. Not that it was uncommon for an alcoholic to relapse. She'd only seen Jake at a couple of meetings, so it wasn't as if she knew him well. There was no good reason for her to be taking this so personally.

"Hey!" Nick appeared at her side, blocking her view of the other man. "You okay?"

"'Course." Not remotely. "Just trying to help out."

"Mamamamama," the little bundle in her arms chanted. Pam wasn't sure if it was random phonetic babbling or a specific request. Mrs. Stein had mostly calmed down her other daughter and was helping her to her feet.

The beleaguered mother tried to smile at Pam. "Thank you so much. I've got it from here."

"You sure?"

She nodded.

After she'd passed the child back and wished

Mrs. Stein well, Pam went straight to Jake Stein, without stopping for any kind of explanation to Nick. She ripped the bottle out of his hands with enough force that some of the contents sloshed across her sleeves and torpedoed it into a nearby garbage can.

Then, with tears stinging her eyes, she raced for the ladies' room, hoping she could get there before she made an even bigger scene than the wailing toddlers.

Nick texted his sister that something had come up and could she please keep an eye on Faith for the rest of the game. Minor medical emerg. in crowd, trying to assist. He just hoped Leigh didn't come to the ladies' room or he was going to be stuck trying to explain why he was pacing outside it, refusing to leave until Pam came back and he could make sure she was all right.

What the hell happened?

They'd been going for a couple of colas, she'd been bumped and the next thing he'd known, she was sprinting down the sidewalk toward the family that had just passed and there were tears and blood and she was throwing some guy's drink.

She'd only been gone a few minutes, but he

felt clueless, which was irritating and made the time pass slower. He was reversing direction for another lap when she emerged, red-eyed and sheepish.

"You want to tell me what that was about?" he asked gently. She didn't look like she needed an impatient interrogation.

"That guy who dropped his daughter? He was drinking. And he shouldn't have been," she said.

"Okay." He supposed that made sense. It surprised him a bit that she'd become so emotional over it, although he had to admit that the sight of blood on that poor little girl's face had left even him shaken. And he was astute enough to realize that Pam's own personal issues had magnified her response.

She sighed. "I don't mean to ruin your evening, but do you think you could take me home? I wasn't feeling that great when I got here, and now..."

"Yeah, okay." He could probably make it back before the end of the game, but if it looked like he wouldn't, he'd call his sister. "Guess I'm ready whenever you are."

She was quiet on the walk through the parking lot, the only sound coming from her the jangling rattle of the charms on that silly mum he'd bought. It had seemed like a cute idea at the time, but now it made him wince. Tonight just didn't seem like the right venue for silly. In the background, the band led the crowd in the "Charge!" cheer and Nick cast about for something to say.

Halfway to her house, he still hadn't come up with much. He told her that he was looking forward to meeting Bryce's parents when they picked up Faith for the dance tomorrow night and that he had narrowed down Faith's Christmas present to three guitars and would love to get Pam's opinion before he made his purchase. All of this was met with semiaudible, monosyllabic responses.

Rolling up to the house in the dark, the two of them alone in the car, brought on a serious case of déjà vu. How many times had he brought her home after Friday night football games?

Since she didn't seem to be in the right frame of mind for nostalgia, he said simply, "I'm worried about you."

"You and me both." She ran a hand through her stylishly choppy hair. "I was standing there with one shrieking kid in my arms, staring at another wailing kid smeared in her own blood, and I thought, 'I need a drink.'"

Was that why the waterworks afterward?

"Lots of people would have that same reaction under those circumstances. But you took that bottle away from the guy and tossed it, you didn't take it from him and start doing shots."

She made a noncommittal noise and opened her door. He followed her up the sidewalk, wishing he knew what she was thinking. Sometimes he felt like he knew her better than anyone else on the planet; other times she'd shocked him— like when she left.

With that long-ago blow in mind, he looked at her living room with fresh eyes. All of the improvements he'd been applauding her for now looked sinister. He thought about the mood she'd been in all evening, the pensiveness in her expression when she met him at the stadium entrance.

"You're finished, aren't you?" he said. "With the house."

She nodded, not looking at him. "It isn't perfect, but most homes that go on the market aren't. It's good, though."

"Are you..." He stopped, swallowed, tried again. "Are you going to stick around until after it sells?"

She sat on the couch, tucking one leg under her. "Technically I don't have anywhere I have to be, although Annabel thinks she's ready for a change of scenery and we've talked about being roommates. The longer I stay here, the harder it will be to leave."

"Then don't leave." He knew it was a mistake even before he said it—she'd see it as pressuring her, and she was having a lousy night. But he couldn't help it. "Would it be so bad to stay?"

"I'm at a good place with Mimosa right now," she said. "Best I've ever been. You follow sports. Don't they always tell athletes to go out while they're on top, retire at the zenith of their game? I'd rather leave town now and never see any of these people again than…than do what that man did tonight. I'd be surprised if his wife stays with him after this."

It was the choice she'd made twelve and a half years ago all over again, he realized. If she convinced herself that it was in their—his, Faith's, her family's—best interest for her to go, she'd probably be out of the town limits before he even got to say goodbye. Then she'd been motivated by her depression and the specter of her dysfunctional relationship with Mae, afraid of how both those things could harm their daughter. Now she was terrified of what would happen if she started drinking again.

He knelt in front of her, taking both her

hands in his. "You're sober now, Pam. I believe in you."

"Which I appreciate," she said, "but you never saw me at my worst. You don't have any real frame of reference. You've only ever seen me sober, but I'm an alcoholic, Nick."

"It's part of who you are, but it's not *what* you are. You're more than that, and you're more than your mother." He got to his feet, frustrated that he wasn't reaching her. The last time she'd left, he'd never had a chance to talk her out of the decision. He couldn't blow this. "You said yourself, you left because you didn't want to be like her, but that's who you became anyway. Running doesn't solve anything."

"I'm not running," she protested tiredly. "I'm moving on because it's time. You knew that was always the plan."

"Damn it, it's a stupid plan! I love you, and I think you love me. And Faith—"

"Don't." Pam held up a hand. "Don't use her to try to guilt me into staying."

He clenched his fist around his car keys. "Are you even going to say goodbye to her before you go?"

"You make it sound like I'm jumping in the car right now. I'm just trying to decide, rationally and unsentimentally, where to go from here. I'm not leaving in the dead of night."

He raised an eyebrow. *You sure about that?*

"Go home," she ordered. "I'm too tired to fight with you and, frankly, it's my life. I don't have to defend my decisions."

"Fine. Whatever you decide, have the guts to tell me? I don't want to read it in a note this time." He went to the door but, before he stepped back out into the night, offered her one last observation to consider. "You know, if you keep pushing away people who love you, you'll wind up *exactly* like Mae. Alone."

It was one of the world's oldest and most annoying paradoxes—being so tired you couldn't sleep. Pam punched her pillow even as she acknowledged defeat. She wouldn't be nodding off anytime soon.

What she really wanted to do was call the hospital and ask if that little girl had been okay, but the staff wasn't allowed to give out information like that. Still, she grabbed her cell phone and checked the time. Just a little after midnight.

She bit her lip. Martha was constantly handing out her number at meetings, saying that she was a chronic insomniac and could be called on around the clock if someone needed to be talked off the ledge. Pam wasn't exactly out on the ledge—more like standing just inside the window, trying to gauge the distance down— but she sure could use a friendly ear. She sent a text, figuring that would be less intrusive if Martha actually had gone to bed. It's Pam. Rough night. U still up?

Her phone rang a moment later. *Guess that answers that question.* "Martha?"

"Oh, hon, I heard about the football game. I've been thinking about you. Need to talk? We can either chat on the phone or meet at the Pie House on Welbington. They're open twenty-four hours and they have a fantastic coconut cream."

"I can meet you in fifteen minutes," Pam said. Less, if she wore flip-flops and didn't brush her hair.

An hour later, both women had polished off sizable pieces of pie and Pam had poured out everything from noticing Jake's glassy eyes and dulled expression to throwing Nick out of her house.

"I've been up front with him," she defended herself. "He always knew I was leaving."

"Mmm," Martha said, sipping her coffee. "Are you siding with him?"

"Course not. But does he have a point? Are you just too afraid to try?"

"Hell, yes. We've been seeing each other for a few weeks, and he's saying *love* and *stay*. He wants long-term commitment. How am I supposed to promise happily ever after when I'm still trying to take it one day at a time? And I certainly can't ask a twelve-year-old to take it one day at a time." She changed the subject. "How well do you know Jake's family?"

"Not well enough that Tami thought to call me after what happened, but enough that she won't mind if I bring a lasagna to the family tomorrow and see how they're doing."

Pam shook her head. "I just keep seeing his little girl's face in my mind." Which was probably why she couldn't sleep. "I've heard him talk about his family at meetings. He loves them. He's got more incentive to try than anyone I know! If he can't do it…"

"Apples and oranges, hon. Just because Jake had a weak moment doesn't mean you will. Or that I will. It's all unrelated."

"I know. Rationally I know you're right. But the statistics are scary."

Martha reached across the table to pat her hand. "*Life* is scary, hon. Don't mean we stop living."

* * *

The rather burly night manager of the Pie House walked both women out to their cars, admonishing them to drive carefully and making one last offer of coffee for the road if either of them felt tired.

On the contrary, Pam was wide-awake, her mind abuzz with everyone's opinions. Even Julia had weighed in with her two cents earlier in the week, saying that she thought Faith was an absolute doll and that nothing would make Julia happier than to see Pam reunited with her ex-husband and daughter.

Now that Pam was sober and her evenings were no longer marked with people arguing with her to hand over her car keys, she found a soothing freedom in driving. Sometimes just being behind the wheel helped her think more clearly. So she meandered around Mimosa for nearly an hour. At one point, she even considered going to the cemetery and watching the sunrise there. She'd refreshed the flowers at her mother's grave several times now, and with each trip, the emotional turmoil she'd felt after that first visit had lessened.

Maybe because coming home to Mimosa had ceased to be about Pam being someone's daughter. In the hours she'd spent with Faith, strumming guitar and talking about boys, she'd glimpsed what it was to be a mom. Could she really walk away again, knowing how much she'd already missed and what she'd be sacrificing? Faith was only at the beginning of her dating years; it was a given that her aunt Leigh and grandma Gwendolyn weren't going to give her straight answers about boys!

And Nick…

Just the image of his face made her heart hurt. The man must be a glutton for punishment. Falling for her the first time had been understandable—he'd been young, stupid and at the mercy of guy hormones. What was his excuse this time? If she left, would he find someone simpler and safer to love, or would he be too embittered to try again? *Three strikes.*

The palest fingers of pink were streaking the sky by the time she turned onto her road. She recalled the way she'd felt when she first jostled down this driveway in August, choked with dread and uncertainty about what to do. Now, whenever the little house came into view, she felt…content.

My mother never could make this place a home, not in all the years she lived here. Mae hadn't had enough love in her to do that. Was it remotely possible that Mae had left her the house hoping that Pam could?

Instead of driving all the way into the carport, Pam parked midway down the gravel stretch. She leaned forward and watched the sun come up over the roof and grinned at the view, pride swelling inside her. *Mine.* Maybe her past here hadn't been pretty, but the present included family, friends and accomplishment. And the future?

She swallowed hard. Well, she'd have to discuss that part with Nick. At least this time she was brave enough to give him a say in the decision.

When Pam knocked, Faith was the one who opened the front door, her face puckered in concern. "Hey! What happened last night? You guys disappeared before kickoff and then Dad didn't want to talk this morning. You didn't have a fight, did you?"

"We had a difference of opinion," Pam said. "Is he around?"

"Backyard, mowing. You want to wait in the kitchen while I go get him?"

"Sure." Since Pam's throat had gone as dry as cracked desert floor, she poured a glass of water and knocked half of it back in one gulp.

"Liquid courage?" Nick asked from behind her.

She spluttered, then had to surreptitiously wipe moisture from the corner of her mouth. *Very smooth.* "No, I have to get my courage the old-fashioned way these days—faking it."

He leaned against the kitchen counter, eyeing her coolly. It was ridiculous for a man to look that good in an orange T-shirt and a pair of cut-off sweatpants. He was handsome as the devil, but all the passion was missing. This was the man who'd shown up at Trudy's to warn her she had no business in Mimosa, not the man who'd trickled corn starch over her bare flesh or raged at her about his daughter's haircut.

Oh, Nick. Seeing how guarded he was, she realized that he was every bit as scared as she was.

She'd meant to explain that she wanted to give this a chance, that she wouldn't leave Mimosa but that she couldn't rush into anything, either. That they were going to have to take it one day at a time for the foreseeable future and just hope that path took them where they wanted to go. Instead, she stared into his shuttered eyes and blurted, "You were right."

"What?" The impassive mask fell away. Shock and tender vulnerability lay beneath it.

"You were right," she repeated. "I do love you."

"Yes!" A high-pitched whoop came from the next room.

Nick pressed the heel of his hand to his head. "I'd send her upstairs, but it seems too late for that to do any good."

Pam sighed. "I suppose she can come join the conversation if it's all right with you. After all, this affects her, too."

Faith skidded into the room in her socks so quickly that she almost crashed into the refrigerator. "Are you staying? You're staying in Mimosa!"

Pam nodded, her eyes locked on Nick. "I'm staying."

He crossed the kitchen in two strides and pulled her in for a deep kiss.

After a minute, Faith tittered. "Guys? I'm totally on board with celebrating the good news, but...*ew.*"

Nick angled back, resting his forehead against Pam's. "We're squicking out our daughter," he whispered.

"Squicking?"

"I'm told it's a word." He tightened his embrace around her as if disbelieving she'd stay of her own volition. "You're really not leaving?"

"No. I worked too damn hard on that house to go just when it's getting good."

"It'll get even better," he swore. "I'll get you a dishwasher for Christmas. Top of the line!"

She laughed, but then pulled back so that she could think clearly enough to articulate what needed to be said. "I want to promise you that I'll never touch another drink, that I won't panic and freak out at the thought of permanent commitment, but…"

"Pam, you're one of the strongest people I know," he told her. "Even when you bolted before, you acted out of a sense of integrity. And you were a kid! That's not going to happen again. If you ever did happen to fall off the wagon, we'd find a way to cope with it and move forward."

Her vision blurred. "You think?"

His own eyes were damp with emotion, too. "I know. Hey, it's not like you get off so easy. You'll have to deal with my grouchy, hotheaded temper when I get angry and act irrationally. And what about the times when this one behaves like a brat?" He jerked his thumb toward his daughter.

"Hey!" But she was grinning from ear to ear, pleased to be included.

"As long as you both understand that we

can't rush into anything," Pam cautioned. "No crazy talk of people moving in together or getting married."

"No, not yet!" Faith yelped, looking harried. "You know how long it will take me to write the perfect song to sing at the wedding? Not to mention working up the courage to perform in front of people. And a person doesn't learn to play guitar overnight!"

Pam looked from the love of her life to their daughter and smiled. "Don't worry, we've got time."

Most importantly, they had each other.

* * * * *

YES! Please send me **The Hometown Hearts Collection** in Larger Print. This collection begins with 3 FREE books and 2 FREE gifts in the first shipment. Along with my 3 free books, I'll also get the next 4 books from the Hometown Hearts Collection, in LARGER PRINT, which I may either return and owe nothing, or keep for the low price of $4.99 U.S./ $5.89 CDN each plus $2.99 for shipping and handling per shipment*. If I decide to continue, about once a month for 8 months I will get 6 or 7 more books, but will only need to pay for 4. That means 2 or 3 books in every shipment will be FREE! If I decide to keep the entire collection, I'll have paid for only 32 books because 19 books are FREE! I understand that accepting the 3 free books and gifts places me under no obligation to buy anything. I can always return a shipment and cancel at any time. My free books and gifts are mine to keep no matter what I decide.

262 HCN 3432 462 HCN 3432

Name	(PLEASE PRINT)	

Address		Apt. #

City	State/Prov.	Zip/Postal Code

Signature (if under 18, a parent or guardian must sign)

Mail to the **Reader Service:**

IN U.S.A.: P.O. Box 1867, Buffalo, NY. 14240-1867
IN CANADA: P.O. Box 609, Fort Erie, Ontario L2A 5X3

* Terms and prices subject to change without notice. Prices do not include applicable taxes. Sales tax applicable in NY. Canadian residents will be charged applicable taxes. This offer is limited to one order per household. All orders subject to approval. Credit or debit balances in a customer's account(s) may be offset by any other outstanding balance owed by or to the customer. Please allow 4 to 6 weeks for delivery. Offer available while quantities last. Offer not available to Quebec residents.

Get 2 Free Books,
Plus 2 Free Gifts—
just for trying the Reader Service!

Get 2 Free Books,
Plus 2 Free Gifts—
just for trying the Reader Service!

Get 2 Free Books,
Plus 2 Free Gifts—
just for trying the
Reader Service!

Get 2 Free Books,
Plus 2 Free Gifts—
just for trying the
Reader Service!

YES! Please send me 2 FREE Harlequin® Heartwarming™ Larger-Print novels and my 2 FREE mystery gifts (gifts worth about $10 retail). After receiving them, if I don't wish to receive any more books, I can return the shipping statement marked "cancel." If I don't cancel, I will receive 4 brand-new larger-print novels every month and be billed just $5.49 per book in the U.S. or $6.24 per book in Canada. That's a savings of at least 19% off the cover price. It's quite a bargain! Shipping and handling is just 50¢ per book in the U.S. and 75¢ per book in Canada.* I understand that accepting the 2 free books and gifts places me under no obligation to buy anything. I can always return a shipment and cancel at any time. Even if I never buy another book, the 2 free books and gifts are mine to keep forever.

161/361 IDN GLQL

Name _____ (PLEASE PRINT) _____

Address _____ Apt. # _____

City _____ State/Prov. _____ Zip/Postal Code _____

Signature (if under 18, a parent or guardian must sign) _____

Mail to the **Reader Service:**
IN U.S.A.: P.O. Box 1867, Buffalo, NY 14240-1867
IN CANADA: P.O. Box 611, Fort Erie, Ontario L2A 9Z9

Want to try two free books from another line?
Call 1-800-873-8635 today or visit www.ReaderService.com.

* Terms and prices subject to change without notice. Prices do not include applicable taxes. Sales tax applicable in N.Y. Canadian residents will be charged applicable taxes. Offer not valid in Quebec. This offer is limited to one order per household. Books received may not be as shown. Not valid for current subscribers to Harlequin Heartwarming Larger-Print books. All orders subject to credit approval. Credit or debit balances in a customer's account(s) may be offset by any other outstanding balance owed by or to the customer. Please allow 4 to 6 weeks for delivery. Offer available while quantities last.

Your Privacy—The Reader Service is committed to protecting your privacy. Our Privacy Policy is available online at www.ReaderService.com or upon request from the Reader Service.

We make a portion of our mailing list available to reputable third parties that offer products we believe may interest you. If you prefer that we not exchange your name with third parties, or if you wish to clarify or modify your communication preferences, please visit us at www.ReaderService.com/consumerschoice or write to us at Reader Service Preference Service, P.O. Box 9062, Buffalo, NY 14240-9062. Include your complete name and address.

Get 2 Free Books,
<u>Plus</u> 2 Free Gifts –

just for trying the Reader Service!

STRS17

Get 2 Free Books,
Plus 2 Free Gifts—
just for trying the Reader Service!

HARLEQUIN® ~Western Romance

READERSERVICE.COM

Manage your account online!

- Review your order history
- Manage your payments
- Update your address

> ### We've designed the Reader Service website just for you.

Enjoy all the features!

- Discover new series available to you, and read excerpts from any series.
- Respond to mailings and special monthly offers.
- Browse the Bonus Bucks catalog and online-only exculsives.
- Share your feedback.

Visit us at:

ReaderService.com